Raul watched Emma

He'd seen her before, but each time he found himself surprised by her appearance. The tall, thin blonde hadn't been what he'd expected. There was a hint of uncertainty, a slight hesitation in her manner. It wasn't a detail anyone else would have noticed, but Raul had spent the past few years looking for people's weak spots. He'd had to learn that skill because his life depended on it.

When he was ready to approach her, Raul moved away from the bar, threading his way through the crowd. And that was when he saw William Kelman.

Kelman was working the room, heading inexorably toward Emma. Raul had hoped all along this encounter would happen—had counted on it—but now that it was, the reality turned his stomach. Seeing Kelman approach her was like watching a snake stalk a mouse.

Raul grabbed a bottle of beer from a nearby waiter and told himself it didn't matter. He had a job to do and nothing else was important. Emma Toussaint was Kelman's mouse—and the reason Raul was there.

He and Kelman were two of a kind. Users. Predators. Men who took what they wanted and never looked back. In his other life, Raul had been a peaceable, law-abiding person, but all that had changed because of William Kelman. Now they were the same.

The realization should have made Raul unhappy. In his other life, it would have.

Dear Reader,

Obsession is set in Santa Cruz, Bolivia, a place I visited frequently a few years back when Pieter, my husband of twenty-five years, lived and worked there. The locale proved irresistible to me. Despite its overwhelming poverty, Bolivia is a place of beauty and hidden treasures. The longer I stayed, the more I realized I had to set a book in Santa Cruz. The city is lovely and the people even more so. Friendly and open, they are terribly interested in everything American.

In the course of my travels, however, I've learned that no matter how attractive the location, most Americans still long for home. They miss their loving families, their familiar haunts, even their fast-food restaurants.

Emma Toussaint is no different but she has a special reason for feeling this way. Forced from her job and divorced by an unloving husband, Emma has lost the right to see her children. She has only one phone call a week during which to hear their precious voices. She goes to Bolivia knowing she may never see them again, but hoping otherwise. Her hero, Raul Santos, is there for a totally different reason. He wants revenge. When their paths cross, neither will ever be the same again.

I hope you enjoy your "visit" to Bolivia and that you'll love the two new friends you'll make—Emma and Raul—as well!

Sincerely,

Kay David

P.S. In January 2001 watch for *The Negotiator*, the first book in my upcoming trilogy about a courageous SWAT team located on the Emerald Coast of Florida.

Obsession
Kay David

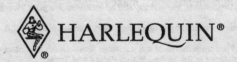

HARLEQUIN®

TORONTO • NEW YORK • LONDON
AMSTERDAM • PARIS • SYDNEY • HAMBURG
STOCKHOLM • ATHENS • TOKYO • MILAN • MADRID
PRAGUE • WARSAW • BUDAPEST • AUCKLAND

ISBN 0-373-70945-5

OBSESSION

Copyright © 2000 by Carla Luan.

This edition published by arrangement with Harlequin Books S.A.

® and TM are trademarks of the publisher. Trademarks indicated with ® are registered in the United States Patent and Trademark Office, the Canadian Trade Marks Office and in other countries.

Visit us at www.eHarlequin.com

Printed in U.S.A.

Major Stan Clark of the Texas Department of Highways
provided invaluable insight for this book.
I'd like to thank him and acknowledge his help.
Texas is a great state because of men like Major Clark.

As always, a special thank-you goes to Heather, Pat
and Marilyn, too. Great writers and even better friends.

CHAPTER ONE

Santa Cruz, Bolivia

TWO YEARS, three months, seven days.

Staring out the smudged and dirty window of her taxi, the cobbled streets and crowded sidewalks passing by in a blur, Emma Toussaint wondered if the day would ever come when she would stop keeping track of time. When she would no longer look at a calendar and automatically calculate the number of weeks that had passed since her life— as she had known it—had ended. She doubted it would. Adding up the days was as natural to her now as breathing.

She tried not to dwell on the situation, but in moments like these, when she had to do something she didn't really want to do, her past came back full force, and it was impossible to ignore. All that occupied her mind was what she no longer had.

Her family. Her home. The life she'd worked so hard to create.

As if he was deliberately trying to distract her, the driver plunged the vehicle into the melee of the

First Ring, the taxi's bumper barely missing the fender of the ancient truck in front of them. The city streets were laid out in a series of concentric circles, and the congestion never ended. Emma grabbed for the door handle, then realized too late it was missing. With a *swoosh,* she slid across the cracked leather seat to the other side.

She shook her head and held on to her purse a little tighter. The taxis in Santa Cruz were like everything else in this part of South America. Rundown and just getting by. For as long as she'd been in Bolivia, two years now, the whole country had seemed on the edge of collapse—a state with which she could easily sympathize.

The beat-up Toyota she was in whipped out of the traffic circle and merged onto Avenida de Ventura, the main street of Santa Cruz. It was after eight in the evening and the area was still crowded and noisy, exhaust and smoke hanging over the thoroughfare in a dirty brown cloud. Most of the cars packed around her were ancient and filthy, with gaping cavities in the passenger-side dashboard. She'd been here four months before her Spanish had been good enough to ask about the disconcerting holes. She'd learned then that the vehicles had come from Japan where they'd been right-hand drives. Ripping out the steering wheels, exporters adapted the cars, then shipped them to Bolivia. The autos had spent the prime of their lives in another country and had come here on the downswing.

Just like most of the people.

The driver barreled past four stop signs, honking, then blasting straight into the intersections without hesitating. A block later, he jerked the car to a stop at a light he couldn't ignore.

Thinking of the party she was going to at the Taminaca Bar—*dreading* the party she was going to—Emma turned her attention away from the traffic and gazed out the side window. Quickly she realized her mistake and looked the other way, but not quickly enough. Her brain registered what she didn't want to see, and her heart swelled with sympathy and pain.

The Quechua Indian woman who stood on the corner, every day, rain or shine, cold or hot, was there. Emma went down this street, Ayacucho, on her way to work, and she always saw her. She could see the *India* begging from her office window, as well.

The poor woman couldn't have been much older than thirty, but she looked twice that. Her skin was like leather, toughened by daily exposure to the sun and wind. She wore a short-brimmed felt hat—the green one today, not the brown. Underneath it, her black hair hung in two thick plaits, which fell well past her waist. The strands were threaded with gray—from the dust or simply premature aging,

Emma couldn't tell. The rest of her outfit was the same; it never changed from one day to the next, except that she sometimes wore long pants beneath the four skirts she wore. Also three blouses, a vest, endless petticoats—more layers of clothing than Emma could generally count. And then there was the *aguayo*. Using every color of the rainbow, the fragile shawl was frayed and torn, mended so much Emma was continually shocked to see it still in one piece. As usual, the woman had knotted it behind her neck and then slung it diagonally across her chest. Each village wove a different pattern; if you recognized the design, you could tell where the owner came from.

Holding her breath, Emma looked at the *aguayo*.

The child was there, bundled up so tightly inside the rag it couldn't move anything but its eyes. Two black dots stared back at Emma from beneath a thatch of equally dark hair. A smudge of something white was on the baby's cheek.

A physical catch formed inside Emma's throat, closing it down as tightly as if fingers were wrapped around her neck and squeezing. She struggled against the sensation and tried to swallow, but the feeling wouldn't go away. She almost wished someone *was* trying to strangle her. Then her brain would shut down, too, and she wouldn't have to think anymore.

That wouldn't happen, though. Emma had seen

the Quechua too many times and had hoped for that same kind of relief without it coming. There was *always* a child in the *aguayo*. Sometimes older, sometimes younger, but always there was a child. And seeing it always affected her just this way.

Without meaning to, Emma found herself leaning toward the car window, her palm flat against the glass, her fingers spread, almost as if she was reaching out for the baby. The pain in her chest spread in a wider circle and hampered her ability to think—but not to remember.

Sarah had been eight months old when Emma had left the States, just about the age of the child in the serape. Her eyes had been brown, too, and the fuzz on her head dark and curly. Almost five, Jake had looked more like Emma. Lighter eyes. Blond hair. When she'd brought Sarah home from the hospital, Jake had wanted to hold her. As usual, Todd had protested, but Emma had ignored her husband and carefully situated the little boy on the couch. She'd then lowered the infant into his arms, and when she'd stood up and looked at those precious children, the image had burned itself in her heart. She hadn't understood, beyond the obvious, why it had fixed itself so firmly in her mind at that time. But then again, maybe she had. On a subconscious level, she'd been waiting for disaster for years. Todd had married her and brought her into his life, one completely different from her own, and it'd felt too good to be true right from the very beginning. Not to worry about money. Not to ever think twice about food, shelter or whatever else her children needed. Then everything had changed horribly, almost overnight.

The light went from red to green and the taxi roared down the street, the tiny dirty child and its begging mother falling behind. Emma turned and stared out the back window, but the glass was covered with grit and she couldn't see them. Her heart shuddering, she faced the front once more, then tilted her head against the splintered leather seat and closed her eyes.

Two years, three months, seven days.

RAUL SANTOS leaned against the bar and sipped his cold Paceña, the bitter bite of the beer as it rolled over his tongue and filled his mouth such a pleasure he could hardly believe it. All his senses were heightened. The feel of the wood against his back, the scent of the flowers sitting on a nearby table, even the painting over the mirror by the liquor bottles. The colors looked brighter than they should have, the images more real. The Taminaca Bar in Santa Cruz, Bolivia, was so far removed, so incredibly different, from where he'd been six months ago, it was unnerving.

It almost seemed as if the past five years had happened to someone else.

Almost.

He drained the beer, set the empty bottle on the bar and nodded for another, his thoughts turning harder. Those years *had* happened to someone else. The young idealistic Raul Santos he had been before he'd been sent to prison *was* a completely different person from the man resting against the bar now. They shared the same name, but that was all. His mind, his body, his very soul had been taken out, torn into pieces and reassembled into something totally opposite.

Raul's gaze roved the bar. It was an open-air place, but elegant, with white tablecloths and candlesticks. A blue pool, surrounded by hibiscus plants with enormous red and yellow blossoms, sparkled on the other side from where he stood. At each end of the pool, hammocks were suspended between palm trees. They swayed gently in the evening breeze, and the chatter of wild birds, contained in several cages along the walkway, filled the relative quiet. The place was beginning to fill with women in tight dresses and men in dark suits, arriving one after another. Someone started some salsa music and the pulsing beat drowned out the birds.

At the opposite end of the polished wooden bar, the bartender uncapped two more Paceñas for a black-jacketed cocktail waitress. Without turning her head, she eyed Raul. He eyed her back, his body responding before he could even think twice. There was something about South American women, he thought. The long black hair, the curvaceous bodies, the way they held themselves. He'd traveled to Buenos Aires once—in his other life—and the women there had been the same. Incredible. As she swished away, Raul stared at her backside and wondered if it was something they learned or if it was simply in their genes.

He turned to pick up his drink, and the bartender was waiting, wiping a white rag over the mahogany expanse between them. The man nodded toward the doorway leading out to the interior of the hotel. *"Esa es la señorita. Allá."*

The bartender's Spanish was different from the Spanish Raul had learned as a child in Texas, but not *that* different. He turned and looked. The woman he'd been waiting for stood on the threshold.

He palmed the *bolivianos* he'd tucked under his drink earlier and pushed the bills toward the bartender. Afraid he might miss her, Raul had wanted a second pair of eyes looking for the banker. *"Muchas gracias, señor."*

"De nada." The man's dark eyes gleamed. *"La señorita—es muy bonita, ¿no? Buena suerte, señor…"*

Good luck? Raul nodded his thanks at the man's sentiment, but he didn't need it. He made his own luck.

Turning away, Raul focused on the woman. Emma Toussaint. He'd seen her before, of course, but each time he found himself surprised by her appearance. The tall thin blonde hadn't been what he had expected, although he wasn't able to explain exactly why. Tonight she wore a sleeveless black dress, straight and severe with a scarf tucked into the neckline. She'd probably read in a magazine somewhere that the square of silk would make the dress into a cocktail outfit. She'd been wrong to think so. It still looked like a banker's dress. No nonsense. Businesslike. Boring.

His eyes went to her face. The first time he'd seen her, he'd decided her features were too interesting to be called pretty. Her cheekbones were so high they shadowed the strong-looking jaw beneath, and her nose was too straight and bladelike for conventional beauty. Her hair, falling straight to her shoulders, was glossy and smooth, her eyes hazel and cool. Only her lips seemed out of place. Full, lush and a red that had to be natural, they looked as if they were made to be tasted.

There was something about her, something elusive he couldn't put a name to. She wore a hint of uncertainty, a slight hesitation in the way she held her shoulders. It wasn't a detail anyone else would have noticed, but Raul had spent the past few years looking for people's weak spots. He'd learned the skill because his life had depended on it. Now it was second nature.

As he watched, Reina Alvarado came up and greeted Emma. Kisses were exchanged and they began a conversation. The other woman was as conservatively dressed as Emma, but clearly a local. With dark hair and features, she had a fuller figure and gestured wildly as she spoke. She tottered on four-inch heels, too, a definite South American fashion trend. They were friends, he already knew, very good friends, and Emma obviously felt comfortable around her, some of the tension easing from her body as they talked.

He picked up his drink, biding his time. He wasn't in a hurry. He'd do this like he did everything now—on his terms. Finishing the beer, he ordered another. The alcohol didn't affect him.

The noise level of the party went up, and within the hour the music was all but impossible to hear above the chattering guests. Raul caught snippets of conversation, some in Portuguese, some in English, most in Spanish. He knew no one there, but several people spoke to him, made party conversation. Bolivians were friendly, courteous people, curious about Americans and always ready to talk business or simply converse. He found himself involved in more discussions than he would have liked. It made it harder to keep Emma Toussaint in his sights.

Her blond hair shone, though, and when Raul was finally ready, a little after midnight, he didn't have any trouble spotting her on the other side of the pool. Moving away from the stool, he threaded his way through the crowd and headed toward the edge of the open air bar. Facing a bank of windows covered in reflective film, he walked parallel to her, his eyes trained on the windows, which were as good as mirrors.

And that was when Raul saw him.

William Kelman.

He was working the crowd, greeting people with a gracious smile and ambling slowly so he could talk to everyone. He blended into the group as though he was born to it. He was heading inexorably toward Emma, and Raul paused to watch the drama unfold. He'd hoped all along that this encounter would happen—had *counted* on it happening tonight—but now that the vignette was unfolding, the image turned his stomach. Seeing Kelman approach her was like watching a snake stalk a mouse.

Raul grabbed another bottle of beer from a passing waiter and told himself it didn't matter. He had a job to do and nothing else was important. Emma Toussaint was William Kelman's mouse, and that was the very reason he, Raul, was there.

He and Kelman were one of a kind. Users. Predators. Men who took what they wanted and never looked back. In his other life, Raul had been a peaceable person, a law-abiding citizen, even a gentleman some might have said, but all that had changed because of William Kelman. Now both of them were the same. Both of them sensed the weak and deceived them for their own advantage.

The realization should have made Raul unhappy.

In his other life, it would have.

"HE'S COMING this way. No! Don't look. Stand still, I'll tell you what he's doing. Smile. Act casual."

Emma tried to follow Reina Alvarado's advice, but it wasn't possible; she had to look. Turning her head, Emma glanced over her shoulder, then faced her best friend once more. "That's him? The older one in the tuxedo?"

Reina nodded. "William Kelman. He's a nice-looking man, isn't he?" She raised a hand to her dark hair and fluffed it up around the crown of her head. "Maybe I can snag him. I'm tired of Miguel and all his problems. Did I tell you what he did last week?"

"No, you didn't. But right now the only man I want to hear about is Mr. Kelman, please."

Reina looked peeved, but only for a second. Nothing ever upset her for long, and that was one

of the reasons Emma loved her friend so much.
She needed the balance in her life that Reina gave
her—the laughter, the jokes, the South American
acceptance that life was what you were handed, not
what you made it. They had met, literally, the day
Emma had gotten off the plane. The bank had arranged for Reina, a local real-estate agent, to pick
up Emma from the airport so they could begin to
look at apartments. In the mass confusion of Viru-
Viru, Reina had taken one look at the exhausted
and obviously drained Emma, and they'd gone
straight to the Yotau Hotel. Reina had checked
Emma in, led her to her suite, then ordered room
service for them both. They'd been friends ever
since, and it'd paid off for Emma in more ways
than one. Reina was a pipeline of information and
gossip.

"What do you need to know?" Reina said now,
her perfect eyebrows arching above snapping black
eyes. "He's rich, he's an American, and he needs
a banker." She poked Emma discreetly in the ribs.
"That's you."

Emma couldn't help but laugh. "Haven't you
already relieved him of that money? Last time we
talked, you said you were taking him to Las Palmas to look at houses."

"I did," Reina said smugly. "And he bought
the biggest one out there. You know, the pink one
on the huge lot with the pool and the garden." She

leaned closer. "It cost a fortune and he didn't blink an eye."

Emma's interest quickened, and she risked another look. William Kelman had stopped to talk to someone, the local consul general, she realized with a start. The woman was smiling and laughing with Kelman as if the two knew each other well. Standing beside them was one of the directors of the embassy. Emma noticed he didn't look quite as happy, but she gave him a passing glance only. She was interested in Kelman.

He wasn't tall, but his military bearing added stature and power to his appearance. He was nearer to sixty than fifty, she estimated, with close-cropped hair almost completely gray. As she watched, he tilted his head toward the consul, and for the first time, Emma realized he had someone with him. A very young, very beautiful woman. Dressed in a gold sheath that revealed a stunning figure, she was standing to one side of Kelman, looking bored, her dark eyes searching the room for something more exciting, her body moving, unconsciously, it seemed, to the music of the band.

"You're staring," Reina hissed. "Turn around. I'll tell you when he's coming this way."

Emma shifted to look at her friend once more, but as she did, she suddenly felt every one of her thirty-five years. The simple black dress she'd selected seemed dowdy. She hadn't taken the time to apply more makeup or fix her hair. Touching the ends of it, she knew there was nothing she could do about it now.

Reina read her mind. "You look perfect," she said. "Just like a banker."

"I know," Emma answered. "I just..." She shook her head. "That girl he's with. She's so young, so gorgeous..." She let her voice die out.

"They're all young and gorgeous, *chica,* but we've got experience. That's more important!"

A moment later William Kelman was at their side, the girl trailing behind him. "Reina!" He leaned over and kissed her. "How's my favorite real-estate agent?"

Reina beamed. "*Muy bien, señor.* And how's your Spanish?"

"It's not improving," he said. "Not one damned bit."

Before he could say anything else, Reina reached out and put her hand on Emma's arm. "This is my friend, Emma Toussaint."

Emma extended her hand and William Kelman took it. He squeezed so hard she felt her ring cut into the flesh of her fingers, but on reflex, she squeezed back, just as forcefully. His eyes narrowed momentarily, then he released his grip.

"So you're the banker, eh? I've heard a lot about you. Your name gets dropped in all the right places."

"I'm glad to hear that." Emma met his eyes and smiled.

"You're at Banco, right?"

"That's correct. I work for Banco Nacional. I'm in charge of their foreign-currency exchanges and expatriate accounts."

"Convince me it's a good idea to put all my money with you and your bank."

She smiled politely. There was a shop downtown that sold Brazilian blue topaz the exact shade of William Kelman's eyes. She'd never liked the stone—its color was cold and impersonal.

"I don't have to convince you," she said. "Talk to my other clients and you'll convince yourself."

His expression didn't change, but she'd dealt with so many men like him back in New Orleans she could tell what they were going to say before they opened their mouths. Like her ex-husband and his family, they had money and they thought it made them special.

"I've already heard everyone's opinions," he said. "But I make up my mind for myself."

"Don't you find that hard to do without the facts?"

He smiled. It was a chilly expression that matched his eyes. "Not really. I find most 'facts' highly overrated."

She made a motion with her head, a quick tilt as if to agree with his witticism. She needed the man's business—there was no reason to make him angry. "We're not the biggest bank in town, Mr. Kelman, but we handle all the important accounts. I'm sure you'd be very happy with us."

"I'll come see you sometime next week." He stuck out his hand. "I assume that's convenient?"

She accepted his grip. This time it was looser, as if she'd passed some kind of test. "I'd be delighted to see you anytime."

He nodded and moved away after kissing Reina on the cheek. Emma took a deep breath and let it out slowly, her shoulders slumping before she could stop herself, relief flooding her now that the moment had passed. She'd come to the party for this one reason—to let William Kelman check her out and obtain a meeting with him. She hoped it was worth it.

Reina grabbed her arm and grinned. "Let's go get another drink," she whispered. "I have a feeling you're going to have something to celebrate soon."

RAUL WATCHED the two women head toward the bar, their business with Kelman obviously concluded. Emma Toussaint appeared more relaxed. Looking down at her friend, she tossed her head and smiled, her blond hair swinging against her neck. Even her step was easier, he noticed, less stiff and anxious. Clearly she was pleased with how the introductions had gone. Raul allowed himself a corresponding flicker of satisfaction, then he searched the room with his eyes and found Kelman to judge his reaction.

The man was in a group of people, laughing and talking. The young woman he'd brought with him was nowhere to be seen. He seemed to be participating in the conversation, but as Raul watched, he realized Kelman's attention was actually focused somewhere else. Raul followed the other man's gaze until he understood. Kelman was studying Emma Toussaint, looking at her with a measuring wariness.

In the past, Raul had always addressed his problems directly. As a well-trained attorney, he'd assess the situation, evaluate his priorities, then put his plan into action, a plan that was usually complicated and involved, yet never beyond the limits of what was legal. He believed in doing things the right way; justice and fairness were always behind him.

But the rules were different now. Kelman had changed them when he'd ruined Raul's life. Honesty and ethics were out the window, replaced by lies and subterfuge.

But Raul could handle them as deceit as deftly as he'd been able to handle truth.

Finishing his beer, he gave the matter no more thought. He put the bottle down and headed across the room. Toward Emma Toussaint.

CHAPTER TWO

RAUL WAS FIVE STEPS from Emma's side when a throng of party goers surged between them. Momentarily thwarted, he had to pause, and when he did, he felt the old familiar prickling sensation along the back of his neck. The one that had saved his life more than once. The one that told him someone had noticed him. Stuck within the center of the throng, he turned. William Kelman was staring directly at him.

All Raul could do was stare back. Sooner or later he'd expected Kelman to know he was in Santa Cruz, so it didn't really matter. But Raul felt his muscles tense as their gazes locked. He'd wondered how he'd react the first time he looked into the other man's eyes. Now he knew. He felt only an empty kind of satisfaction for what he knew was coming. It seemed strange, but that was it. Kelman narrowed his eyes, his expression puzzled.

A second passed, maybe two, and the moment was broken by a waiter coming between them. In that instant, Raul realized Kelman didn't recognize him. For five years Raul had thought of nothing but seeking revenge on this man, and apparently he didn't even remember Raul. Under different circumstances, the situation might have been amusing. For now, all Raul wondered was what this meant to his plans. He decided quickly that if Kelman couldn't place him, all the better.

With the crowd still pressing around him, Raul gave up and let himself be carried down the sidewalk. The entire group spilled outside and began to pile into the taxis lining the street in front of the bar. They were moving on to another location, and even though they were strangers, they began to insist that Raul come with them. Laughing and playing along, he turned them down, then he saw the opportunity. He could connect with Emma Toussaint another time; now it seemed more important to avoid Kelman. A moment later, he was in a cab, driving away with a man and two women, heading for a party he knew nothing about. As they hit the nearby traffic circle, Raul sent a casual glance over his shoulder, back toward the bar. He wasn't surprised at what he saw. William Kelman was standing under the overhang of the bar's entrance, a cigar in one hand, a drink in the other. His eyes were on the departing taxis, and in the dim illumination from a nearby street lamp, his expression was still puzzled.

It wouldn't take him long to figure it out.

EMMA WAS SITTING at her desk on Monday morning when the phone rang. She wasn't reading the currency reports piled in front of her or writing the memo she had due in a few hours; she was just sitting. The party on Saturday night had left her drained, and Sunday had been as awful as it usually was. She lived all week for the moment she could call the States and hear her children's voices, but the minute the telephone conversation was finished, she would feel the force of their absence and break down. The rest of the day was always a painful blur, just hours she had to endure until the next time she could talk to them.

The phone at her elbow sounded again and she reached for it without thinking. The voice at the other end was not one she'd expected, at least not this soon.

"Ms. Toussaint, this is William Kelman. I assume I'm not interrupting anything..."

She sat up straight in her chair. "Mr. Kelman, of course you're not interrupting. I'm glad you called."

"I'd like to discuss my banking situation with you as soon as possible."

"I can see you today." As she spoke, Emma pulled her calendar closer, but she didn't really need to look at it. If Kelman had as much money as Reina said he did, Emma's day was his. "When would you like to come by?"

"That's just it." The hint of reluctance she heard in his voice sounded studied, but Emma told herself she was imagining things. "I can't come in today. Too much going on. I'd like to invite you to dinner, though. Could you meet me at Candelabra, say, around nine?"

Something about the man bothered her and she hesitated, then she chastised herself. There was no good reason she couldn't meet William Kelman for dinner, none whatsoever. She didn't have plans and dinner at Candelabra—the best restaurant in town—was always a pleasure. But more importantly, if she turned down this kind of opportunity and Christopher Evans, her boss, found out, he'd kill her. She'd already told him about meeting Kelman, and Chris was practically frantic to get the man's business.

"Candelabra would be fine," she answered. "I'd be happy to meet you there." She scribbled the notation in her calendar, then pushed it back to the corner of her desk.

"Excellent. Give me your address and I'll send a car."

"That's not necessary," she protested. "I can catch a cab."

"I insist. It's the least I can do for making you work so late."

He wouldn't take no for an answer. By the time she hung up, Emma had given him directions to her home and a promise she'd see him at nine. She felt vaguely uncomfortable, but what did it matter? The man had the potential for becoming a very big client. If she signed him up, they'd be seeing each other a lot. Her customers were the kind who kept a close eye on their money.

Before she could devote more worry to the subject, her phone rang again, her internal line this time.

"Usted tiene una visita."

"Felicity, *Inglés, por favor.*" Emma now spoke perfect Spanish, but she insisted that the secretaries and assistants in her department speak English. People with money were usually paranoid; the clients, mostly British and American, were more comfortable when they could understand what was being said around them. She frowned. It'd been a long time since she'd had to remind the young woman.

"I'm sorry... You have a visitor." Felicity's voice dropped in a way Emma had never heard before. "A gentleman."

"Who is it?"

Felicity gave Emma his name, but it was not familiar, and he didn't have an appointment, either. That was not unusual, though. With the level of wealth most of her clients enjoyed, they expected to drop in and still be welcomed. Emma told the secretary she'd be right out.

She checked her hair and lipstick in a small mirror she kept in her desk, then rose and crossed the carpet. Just outside her private office was a reception area that was exclusive to her clients. They could enter this quarter of the bank through the main lobby or come in by a door that led directly to the street. Emma entered the reception room and looked at her secretary.

Felicity met Emma's eyes and tilted her head toward a man standing near the windows. He had his back to them, his hands locked behind him, but as Emma watched, he turned to face her. A field of energy seemed to surround him, waves of intensity rippling out from where he stood. Emma told herself she was being silly, but she swore she could actually feel the strength of his power from across the room.

She started toward him, her heels clicking on the tile floor. "I'm Emma Toussaint," she said, holding out her hand as she got closer. "How may I help you, Mr. Santos?"

Up close, his magnetism was even stronger. She found herself holding her breath as his dark eyes passed over her in a practiced way. She'd become accustomed to the evaluations of South American males, but the way this man's gaze scanned her body was different. It left her feeling strangely vulnerable. His touch added to the sensation. As they shook hands, it enveloped her with a sizzling heat.

"I'm here to open an account." His voice was low and melodious with a hint of something she couldn't place. "I understand you handle the customers with…special needs."

"I'm in charge of the currency department, and I'm also the vice president of the expatriate accounts." She answered carefully. "On occasion I do help with other areas."

He glanced toward Felicity. The young woman was facing her computer screen with a look of such studied involvement, it was obvious she wasn't missing a word. He turned back to Emma with an amused expression. "Perhaps we could go into your office and I could explain further?"

It wouldn't be the first time a good client had walked in off the street. Never one to turn down an opportunity, Emma nodded, then led the stranger into her office, stopping beside Felicity to order coffee for them both. A moment later Emma was sitting behind her desk and Raul Santos was seated in front of her.

He wasn't really her type, but he *was* an attractive man. Bronzed skin, dark eyes, black hair that gleamed. He was over six feet and clearly not a local. Emma found herself intrigued. Other available men had been in her office since her divorce, but something about this one was different. Maybe it was his intensity. Maybe it was the way he was looking at her with his dark gaze. One way or the other, despite her attraction to him, or maybe because of it, he made her uneasy. She shivered once before she could stop herself and spoke quickly to cover her interest.

"What brings you to Banco Nacional, Mr. Santos?"

He rested his hands on the arms of the chair and looked at her. "Everyone knows about El Banco," he said with a shrug. "It's the only game in town, isn't it?"

"Well, there's a Lloyd's down the street and El Centro, too, but we're the best."

"In your opinion."

She smiled. "In the opinion of all our customers, I'm sure. We *are* the most successful."

"Doesn't that depend on how you define success?"

"I define it as do most of our clients—by a large return on their investments."

"That's what I've heard," he conceded. "And what I'd like, as well."

"So we were recommended, then?"

He nodded. "Yes."

She waited for more—a name, a hint of some sort—but he wasn't going to give it to her. Felicity brought in the coffee, and when she left, he spoke again.

"It doesn't really matter why I chose your bank. What's important is the account I'd like to open."

Ignoring the coffee, he pulled a long black wallet from the inside pocket of his suit. The leather looked smooth and expensive; it matched the rest of him. He withdrew what appeared to be a printed check and pushed it across Emma's desk, along with a business card showing his addresses and phone numbers. "I'll be doing some trading. I think that should cover it."

Emma made no move to pick up the check, but she looked down at it. Drawn from a bank in El Paso, Texas, it gave an amount of seven figures. Before the decimal point. She reached for her phone and hit one button. The door to the office opened immediately, Felicity on the threshold.

Emma motioned her inside, then handed the secretary the check and the card. "Please take care of the paperwork for this." She glanced at the man across the desk. "Will you wait or shall I messenger the documents to you later?"

"How long will it take?"

The bigger the check, the shorter the time. "Ten minutes, maybe fifteen," she said.

"I'll wait."

Felicity nodded and hurried away, a tight grasp on the check as she disappeared out the door. Emma turned back to the man in front of her. Usually she had no trouble visiting with her clients, but for some reason, Raul Santos left her not quite knowing what to say. It felt strange. She hadn't been tongue-tied in years, especially without knowing why.

"What brings you to the area, Mr. Santos? Are you from Bolivia?" *Lame, Emma, really lame.*

"I grew up in Texas, but I've been living in Washington until recently. I moved here to do business. I'm an importer."

Shocked into silence, Emma kept a mask of polite interest on her face. *Importer?* The answer was a standard reply in some circles, but the last one she'd expected from this man. He'd definitely not struck her as being involved in the drug trade, but that was the euphemism everyone in Santa Cruz used for the *narcotraficantes.* "I see," she finally said. "An importer..."

"That's right. I import money." He paused. "And export goods."

"You must be good at it."

He smiled for the first time and something—a quick unexpected reaction—tumbled around inside her chest. "I'm good at what I do, Ms. Toussaint. Very good."

She nodded, uncertain what to say next. Surprisingly he kept the moment from being awkward by turning the conversation to her. "What about you? What brought you to Santa Cruz?"

She hadn't expected the question from him, but Emma had dodged it so many times she had a pat answer ready. "International banking is my specialty. I wanted an opportunity to see the system work.''

''Why here? Couldn't you have done that in the States?''

''I would have spent too many years back home working my way up. I came into Nacional and was quickly promoted to the vice presidency of expatriate accounts. That wouldn't have happened in the States.''

''So you're good at what you do, as well.''

His gaze was dark and unrevealing, but had a pull she couldn't deny. ''Yes, I'm good at it,'' she replied, mimicking what he'd said about himself. ''Very good.''

''Then we'll be a great team.''

His words held an undercurrent of something that only increased her uneasiness, but she smiled. ''Undoubtedly.''

A few minutes later, Felicity returned with the papers. He scanned them quickly, then signed them without questions, obviously familiar with the legal terms. When he finished and rose, Emma escorted him to the door of her office. He stood closer to her than she would have liked, but people did that in South America. She'd learned to live with it. However, being this near to Raul Santos made her all too aware of the custom.

''I'll be traveling a lot, but my base will be here, in Santa Cruz.'' He smoothed a hand down his tie, his fingers strong-looking. No ring. "I'd like to get to know the city. I know it's not part of your job, but could I entice you to dinner this evening to learn more about it?"

He'd managed to surprise her again. "I—I have an engagement already," she said.

"That's too bad," he said. "Perhaps another time?"

Her pulse quickened even though she instinctively knew she should stay away from this man. Something told her he was dangerous. She couldn't afford to upset him, though. She inclined her head and repeated his words. "Another time…"

He acknowledged her answer with a smile, but she wondered if the expression conveyed his true feelings. "I'll be in touch."

She watched him leave, then went back into her office. A second later, a movement outside her window caught her eye, and she walked over to the tinted glass. Raul Santos stood on the corner beside the Quechua woman. He was smiling at her and her child, holding out his hand. The Indian woman snatched at what he offered and ducked her head. A moment after that, he headed down the sidewalk.

Fascinated, Emma looked on as the beggar opened her palm and counted the bills the man had given her. It took her quite a while.

THE ENTRANCE to the restaurant was hidden behind a brick wall and iron gate. When Emma climbed from the car William Kelman had sent her, a valet ran out to the street, unlocked the gate and escorted her into the inner garden. By necessity, Bolivians had tight security, especially in the wealthier neighborhoods such as this one. In fact, Candelabra didn't even look like a dining establishment, so perfectly did it blend in with the surrounding homes. The first time Emma visited, she'd thought the cabdriver had made a mistake and dropped her off at someone's house.

She followed the valet over a small rock-lined walkway bordered by tropical plants. The largest, a beautiful bird-of-paradise, trembled in the night breeze, its red and yellow blooms striking even in the dim lamps near the door. When she stepped into the entrance to the restaurant, she could hear the muted sound of diners.

The maître d' greeted her by name.

"Señorita Toussaint, how beautiful you look tonight!"

Emma smiled at the dark-haired man and replied in Spanish, "Estefan, you flatter me, as always. How are the grandchildren?"

He beamed. "Very well, as always, señorita. Thank you for asking."

Leading her to the table, he continued his chatter until she was seated. "Señor Kelman called and said he would be a few minutes late. He begs your pardon and has ordered champagne for the table.''

Emma seriously doubted that William Kelman had ever begged for anything. Her attention focused, however, on the waiter who had appeared at the maître d's side and was already opening a bottle of champagne. ''None for me,'' she said, putting her hand over her glass.

She hadn't noticed until now, but Estefan already had a flute in his hand. He brought it around and placed it in front of her. It was full of a shimmering gold liquid. Bending closer to her, he rotated the glass to line it up with her plate. ''Ginger ale,'' he pronounced. ''¿Está bien?''

She looked up at him with a grateful expression. ''Muchísimas gracias,'' she said quietly.

''De nada.''

The two men left the table after that, and Emma waited, her fingers wrapped around the thin crystal stem of the glass. She hadn't had a drink since she'd come to Bolivia, and in her business, that wasn't always an easy thing to avoid. The constant parties, the luncheon meetings—everything in Latin American either started or ended with alcohol. She'd been tempted, and always would be, but she hadn't given in. Knowing what she did now, she couldn't risk it, even though she'd already lost all that meant anything to her. One day she'd get her children back, and when she did, no one would be able to point a finger at her.

Sipping the soft drink, she concentrated, instead, on the men and women at the tables around her. In a country where the average daily income was eight dollars, very few locals could afford a meal that easily cost five times as much. Therefore, the people around her were either expatriates or criminals, sometimes both. She greeted a few with a nod of her head. Some were clients, as well.

And Raul Santos? What was he?

He certainly didn't fit the profile of the local drug kings, but in Bolivia, you never knew. The largest homes and the luxury cars couldn't be bought by anyone except those in the trade. Or by Americans, which he claimed to be. She touched the heavy silver knife beside her plate and argued with herself. He really could be a legitimate businessman. The country exported tin and jewelry and had a thriving natural-gas business. A huge sect of Mennonites farmed soybeans in the nearby valley, as well. They had U.S. agents who handled their sales. For all she knew, perhaps he was helping them. She should have set aside her usual reticence and just asked, but she suspected the answer would have been, most likely, not completely truthful.

Raul Santos had the look of a man who kept his secrets. She knew because she had her own.

The arrival of William Kelman a few minutes

later put the other man out of her mind. He shook
her hand and took the seat beside her. Scurrying
over quickly, a waiter filled his champagne glass
from the chilling bottle, and before Emma could
say anything the man filled her flute with champagne, as well. She looked at the glass in dismay,
then adjusted her features immediately.

William lifted his drink for a toast and waited
expectantly. ''To new beginnings,'' he said. ''And
successful ventures.''

Emma brought the glass to her lips and held it
there for a second. Kelman didn't notice that was
all she did. He launched into conversation, bombarding her with questions. By the time their food
arrived, she'd explained Bolivian currency, the
U.S. market and the future of trading in both. He
was a quick study and asked probing questions.
Almost too probing. She was being paranoid, but
something about his cross-examination disturbed
her, and she couldn't pinpoint the reason.

She told herself it might have something to do
with his background. He'd told Reina he'd lived
in Santa Cruz early in his career with the U.S. government. Outside of Washington, D.C., Santa Cruz
had the largest DEA office in existence. Reina
hadn't known for sure, but he must have been an
agent; he definitely had the look of a man who'd
been in law enforcement. He'd loved the town, he
said, and now that he'd retired, without a wife or

family to object, he'd returned to enjoy the warm weather and laid-back atmosphere. Regardless of his explanation, Santa Cruz seemed like a strange choice to Emma. The city was not a place most people would want to spend their golden years.

When they finished their dinner, he waved to the waiter, then without consulting Emma, ordered dessert and brandy. Rising from the table, he looked down at her.

"I have a phone call to make. Would you mind if I excused myself for a moment?"

Under the dim lights of the dining room, his blue eyes looked frostier than they had on Saturday.

"No, of course not," she answered.

He took out a cigar and pointed it at her champagne glass. "You finish that, and I'll be right back."

She'd hoped he hadn't noticed, but obviously he had. Emma watched him disappear toward the rear of the restaurant, then she picked up the flute of champagne and stared at the bubbling wine. She had one goal in life right now: to make as much money as she possibly could so she could hire the best lawyer she could find. That was the only way she'd ever see her children again. And making money meant keeping William Kelman happy.

But she couldn't drink this wine. Alcohol had ruined her life already, stolen from her the very things she valued the most. If Kelman was insulted by her refusal to drink, then he'd just have to be insulted. She needed the money, but she couldn't risk the progress she'd made so far. Nothing was worth that.

Reaching over to a nearby plant, she dumped the glass of expensive champagne into the container. At the very same time, a shadow fell over the table. She looked up to see Raul Santos.

SHE WAS WEARING a sleeveless black dress with a rounded collar. It was as simple and plain as the dress she'd worn on Saturday night, but she'd added pearl earrings and a necklace. In the candlelight, they gleamed almost as richly as her hair. She looked startled to see him.

"Mr. Santos!"

"Please call me Raul," he said. He tilted his head toward the glass in her hand. "Bad wine?"

She glanced down at the empty glass, then back up at him. Her look was steady. "Yes," she lied. "I didn't want to embarrass Estefan."

"Of course." He didn't question her further. It was none of his business, anyway.

"Are you here for dinner?"

"Yes, thanks to your secretary. She recommended this place, you know." *After I read the note in your calendar...*

"I didn't realize that. I'll tell her you approved." Her gaze went to the woman standing beside him, and he knew immediately what she was thinking. Had he already made plans with her when he'd asked Emma out, or had he asked her after Emma had turned him down?

The truth was much simpler. Wendy Fortune was an old friend, and they'd worked together in Washington on several different cases. To everyone else in Bolivia, she was an assistant to the local consul, but her real job was to keep an eye on people who needed watching. She and Raul went back a long way, and part of the path had been personal, too.

He explained none of this, but simply gave Emma her name. The two women shook hands.

"Are you alone?" he asked. "Would you like to join us?"

"I'm with someone," she answered. "But thank you."

They talked a bit more, then the maître d' took them to their own table, a secluded one on the other side of the luxurious dining area, just visible from Emma's own table. Two minutes later, her dining companion returned, pulled out his chair and sat down. This time when William Kelman's eyes met Raul's, instant recognition filled their depths.

From across the room, Raul smiled.

CHAPTER THREE

"DO YOU KNOW HIM?"

William Kelman's voice was cold as he tilted his head to the other side of the room. Without even looking, Emma knew instantly whom he meant.

"Yes, I do," she answered. "His name is Raul Santos."

"Is he a client of yours?"

It wasn't a question she could answer; the people whose money she handled valued their privacy. "My client list is confidential, Mr. Kelman. Surely you appreciate that fact as much as anyone."

He grunted his reply and sipped his brandy, his eyes boring a tunnel across the dimly lit dining room.

After a second, she sneaked a look, too. Raul was meeting William Kelman's stare, and he wasn't blinking. She could almost feel the tension crackling between the two men. Raul's friend Wendy seemed as aware of the silent confrontation as Emma. She reached out and put her hand on his arm and said something quietly. He leaned over to listen, but he didn't break eye contact.

William Kelman looked away first.

"Tell me more about this currency thing," he commanded.

Relieved by his change of subject, Emma took a deep breath. "The local currency is called a *boliviano* and it's equal to one hundred *centavos*."

"What's that in American money?"

"It changes, but on Friday, a *boliviano* was worth about fifty cents, give or take a bit."

"And you make money for your clients by trading this currency, right?"

"That's part of what I do."

"How does that work, exactly?"

"The official exchange rate floats, but it's reviewed periodically. The government has five to ten million dollars they handle every day. I sell *bolivianos* for dollars or vice versa, and if I do it right, I make money on the margin—the difference between the two amounts."

"How do you know how many dollars they'll offer?"

"I don't know," she answered. "But that's not really important. The rate is what counts."

"How much do you make for your clients doing this?"

"It varies from day to day."

"On?"

"On a lot of things. The markets the day before, the movement of the other currencies being traded, the local economy…"

He leaned his elbows on the table, and at the same time Emma felt a hot gaze on her back. Raul Santos was still staring at them, she could tell.

"Do you know the rate ahead of time?"

She looked at him in surprise. "The rate is examined by a government committee. If there is a change, it's secret until it's announced a few days later. For obvious reasons."

"But if you did know the figure in advance, you'd make more money for your clients, right?"

His question was unsettling, but Emma tried to make light of it. "Only until I got caught—which would probably be immediately. If I knew the information in advance and acted on it, that would be insider trading. It's as illegal here as it is in the United States."

He paused, and for some reason, her uneasiness grew. "And you don't break the law, do you, Ms. Toussaint?"

"No," she said, "I don't."

He nodded slowly, but she had the feeling he didn't believe her. "Not for anything?"

She opened her mouth to answer the same way, then she hesitated. She'd make a deal with the devil if it meant getting her kids back. She'd do anything for them, wouldn't she? Even break the law?

Over the middle of the table, she lifted her eyes and their gazes locked. Then he smiled.

RAUL WATCHED William Kelman and Emma depart the restaurant. He'd thought Kelman was going to come over and speak to him, but he hadn't, and Raul had felt a flash of disappointment. He'd almost welcome a direct confrontation, to settle things as he'd done when he was younger and knew less—with fists and bloodied noses. It was a more honest way, but Kelman didn't operate like that. He was sneaky and underhanded, and when this was all over, bloody noses would not be the end result.

Rising from the table, Raul motioned to Wendy to do the same. "Let's go," he said roughly. "I want to follow them. I want to know where she lives."

Wendy stood up, grabbing her purse and coat, while she protested, "This is crazy, Raul. You're heading for disaster."

Taking her elbow, he led her away from the table and shook his head. "Disaster was losing five years of my life to that son of a bitch. What's going to happen next is not disaster."

"And the woman? What do you think she'll call it?"

Ignoring Wendy's question, Raul stopped at the front door and motioned to the valet to bring his car, handing the man a wad of bills. He'd already arranged to have the car nearby, and within seconds they were in it and driving off. Ahead of them, along the boulevard, he could just make out the taillights of the car Emma was in. Kelman had departed in a different one.

As if the conversation had never been interrupted, Wendy spoke again, her voice insistent. "Emma Toussaint is going to get hurt, Raul. And she doesn't deserve it. She'll be an innocent victim, caught up in your scheme for revenge. Doesn't that bother you?"

Raul swerved to avoid a pothole the size of a small crater. They were heading to the First Ring, in the central part of town, an older area shunned by most of the expatriates. "There's no other way," he said grimly. "And she's not that innocent, anyway. I checked her out."

"What do you mean?"

He shook his head impatiently. "It's not important, but believe me, she's had her share of trouble. And she caused most it herself."

"Well, that might be true, but she didn't cause yours. And it's not fair to drag her into this."

"Who said life is fair?"

Wendy shook her head at his cynical reply.

"You should walk away and forget about him, Raul."

"Is that what you would do?"

"Yes, I would, because this isn't worth it. William Kelman is a dangerous man, and you're going to get hurt, maybe killed. To make matters even worse, you're going to take that poor woman with you."

"No one's going to die." He paused. "I just want to make Kelman *wish* he was dead, and the key to that is taking his money. I can't do that without her help."

"And if she doesn't offer it?"

"She will, whether she knows it or not."

There was obviously nothing else she could say, and Wendy fell silent. Ten minutes later, Raul slowed his SUV as the vehicle ahead of them entered a deserted side street and parked, a cloud of exhaust pouring from its tailpipe. The homes were modest, not what he would have expected for an American banker. Emma stepped from the car and hurried to the front gate of a two-story house. It was mostly hidden behind a brick wall covered in some kind of greenery, but from the little Raul could see, it looked well tended. Unlocking the iron entrance, she disappeared from sight. His window down, Raul heard her walking up the sidewalk, then the sound stopped and a moment after that, a door slammed. The finality of the noise didn't faze him. He threw his truck in gear and made a sharp U-turn. Fifteen minutes after that, he was in front of Wendy's house.

"Is there any way I can change your mind?" Wendy reached across the seat and put her hand on his. Her touch was warm and it brought back memories. "Is there any way I can stop you from going back there?"

Beneath the casual tone, Raul heard what she was trying to ask.

"No," he said. "Kelman might show up there later, and I need to know if he does. I have to understand what kind of relationship they have."

He read the disappointment that flashed across her face, even though the expression was gone immediately. She'd expected his answer. She nodded and reached for the door handle, then paused.

"Going back there tonight would be a mistake, Raul," she said softly. "A very big mistake."

He met her troubled gaze with a blank one of his own. "It won't be the first time. Or the last."

BY THE TIME Raul got back to Emma's, it was almost one in the morning. Except for a single low light in one upstairs corner, the house and gardens were dark. He parked the truck, then settled into the expectant stillness to wait.

EMMA RAN THE BRUSH through her hair and absentmindedly looked at her watch. Sarah and

Jake had been asleep for hours, or at least they
should have been. She imagined them in their beds,
tucked in safe and sound. She'd done Sarah's room
in lavender and pink, Jake's in dark green and
navy. Todd had complained when Emma had selected the colors, saying they didn't match the rest
of the house. The decorator had concurred and
been horrified when he'd seen them. But Emma
hadn't cared. Her hand stilled as she remembered
her son's face when he'd first seen the baseball
wallpaper. His eyes had blazed with excitement,
and he'd jumped up and down, squealing with
delight.

Before Emma could stop herself, her vision
blurred with tears. Angrily she threw down the
hairbrush and wiped at her eyes, but it didn't do
any good. The stinging tears continued. She took
a ragged breath, but several minutes passed before
she managed to get a tenuous hold on her emotions. Searching her brain for a distraction, she focused on the first thing she thought of—Raul Santos.

Seeing him at Candelabra this evening had been
a shock. She wasn't sure why—the man obviously
had no trouble getting a date—but she hadn't expected him there, especially with a gorgeous
woman on his arm. They'd talked a lot, their dark
heads together, their hands wrapped around match-

ing glasses of wine. What on earth had he thought
when he'd caught Emma pouring out her glass of
champagne? She couldn't imagine what must have
run through his head, but she told herself she didn't
care. It would have been far worse for her if she'd
drunk the wine.

She stood abruptly and crossed her bedroom to
the window facing the street. Over the garden wall,
the avenue was dark and deserted, save for several
vehicles parked on the other side. A night bird
called out, his cry piercing the empty silence.

After a second she dropped the curtain and
turned. Halfway to her bed, she stopped impulsively and returned to her desk by the window to
flick on her computer. The hard drive whirred into
action as she pointed the mouse to her server icon.

The modem connection clicked and hummed,
then a few seconds later, connected. At the other
end, the phone began to ring and her screen began
to blink. Navigating to the site she needed, Emma
entered her password, then nodded in satisfaction.
Leon was on-line, just as she'd known he would
be.

She imagined him sitting in a trance before his
computer at the bank in New Orleans. The lab op-
erated twenty-four hours a day, and Leon always
took the night shift. Totally without social graces,
he'd managed to insult half the management team
when he'd worked as a summer intern at the bank.

The other half had seen his wardrobe and assumed he was a homeless kid hanging around the lobby to stay cool. She'd sensed the brains behind the facade and had gotten Leon Davis his job; she hoped he remembered that now.

She typed quickly. "Leon, this is Emma Toussaint. I hope I'm not interrupting anything important."

His answer reflected his surprise. "I'm just surfing. Nothing important. What's up?"

There was caution in his short reply, and she wasn't surprised. Todd hadn't just ruined her personal life; he'd annihilated her professional one, as well. Everyone at the bank—even down in the computer lab, she was sure—had heard the gossip. Knowing her ex-husband and his family as she did, she was sure he'd kept the bad news alive as much as he could.

Her fingers tapped out her answer. "I'm working overseas—in South America—and I've got a question. I don't know anyone who could help me but you."

The flattery worked, just as she knew it would.

"I'll give it my best shot."

She paused. He was brilliant and could get the information; she'd been the only person at the bank who hadn't been ready to fire him when they'd discovered he'd hacked his way into the salary file

to see what everyone was making. But how to pose
her query?

"I want you to check out someone for me. Discreetly," she typed. "Raul Santos. He's a new cus-
tomer at my bank. Used to live in Washington,
D.C., or possibly El Paso, Texas." She hit the enter
key before she could think too hard about it.

"Sounds interesting. You want that real time or
can I get back to you?"

"There's no hurry."

"No problem. I'll catch you later in the week.
Stay cool."

She leaned back in her chair and stared at the
monitor. She wasn't sure why she'd done what she
just had. If anyone found out, she'd have a hard
time explaining. Requesting personal data on her
clients was not standard operating procedure. On
the other hand, Raul Santos didn't seem like her
usual client.

If she wanted to check out someone, it ought to
be William Kelman. Any time a client asked the
kind of questions he had this evening, a red light
came on in Emma's brain. Curiosity of that sort
usually meant one thing—the person wanted it for
a reason, and it generally wasn't a legitimate one.
She thought briefly of talking it over with Chris
but just as quickly decided against saying anything
to her boss. He didn't like problems, and anything
remotely out of the ordinary was a problem to him.

She shut down her machine, empty silence replacing the mechanical hum of the computer.

One way or the other, she needed Kelman's account and as many like it as she could find. Each one meant a bonus, and each bonus brought her one step closer to her goal—having enough money to buy the meanest, toughest lawyer New Orleans had to offer. She'd fought Todd with everything she'd had, but that hadn't been enough. When she went back to try again, she'd have what she needed.

Nothing else mattered.

THE DIM LIGHT behind the upstairs window went out at 1:45 a.m. Raul glanced at his watch, then waited five more minutes before starting the truck. He drove slowly down the street toward Emma's house and paused right in front. She didn't know what kind of vehicle he had, so if she looked out the window it wouldn't matter, anyway.

As if the house were breathing, the upstairs curtains moved in and out in a rhythmic pattern. Must be a fan, he thought, something to break the still night air. He wasn't prepared for the image that appeared next in his mind, surprising him with its intensity. Emma in bed. The blond hair shining in the darkness. Her slim body in a nightgown. Her fingers curled against the sheets. In the restaurant this evening, her elegant beauty had made every

other woman in the place look overblown, too
made up.

Then he remembered his words to Wendy.
Emma had had her share of troubles. The file he
had on her back at the villa he'd rented contained
only the barest details, but they were grim. She'd
grown up in Louisiana and met Todd Toussaint at
college. They'd married, and two children had followed quickly—but so had disaster.

Todd Toussaint had made sure everyone knew
the split was not his fault. He divorced her and her
life went downhill quickly. She was fired from the
bank, and he gained full custody of the children.
Without a family, a job or even references, she'd
ended up in Santa Cruz, Bolivia.

Emma Toussaint had nowhere to go and nothing
to lose. She was just the kind of woman William
Kelman would seek out and use.

All Raul had to do was stand by and watch it
happen.

CHAPTER FOUR

THEY MET AT PARQUE URBANO twice a week, where four laps around the track equaled two miles. Reina could keep up with Emma for three circuits, but on the fourth one, she always fell back and Emma would surge forward. They'd connect again at the finish line. On Wednesday morning, as Emma was ending her run, she saw Reina, already sitting on the curb, fanning her face. She rose slowly as Emma neared.

"One more time," Emma urged her, still jogging in place. "C'mon, we'll walk it."

"I can't," Reina puffed. "No way."

"I thought you were interested in a rich husband," Emma teased, finally stopping. "How're you gonna catch one if you can't run after him?"

Reina made a face of disgust. "Good point. I'll go, but you have to bribe me."

Emma took a swig from the water bottle she'd left on a nearby bench. "With what?"

"I want to hear about your dinner with William Kelman."

Emma shook her head and began to walk, Reina

trailing at her side. "You know I can't talk about my clients with you."

"I don't want to know about his bank balance! I meant your dinner, silly."

Emma spoke slowly. "Well, he's...strange. You should have warned me. He asked me all kinds of questions about trading."

"That's your job. Why is it strange for him to ask you about it?"

"Let's just say the questions weren't the kind I usually get," Emma answered. "They were more about how to get around the system than how to use it the way you're supposed to."

"He's been in and out of Santa Cruz for years and never had any trouble. I think he's okay."

"You think he's okay because you're interested in him."

"And why shouldn't I be? He may be old, but he's rich and single. He told me all about himself when I was showing him houses. He was a big shot with the government. He went back and forth between here and the States, doing deals. He's not some *narcotraficante*."

The word made Emma's mind shoot off in a different direction. Toward the man she'd met the other day. She spoke impulsively. "Reina, do you know a guy by the name of Raul Santos? He's an American, too. You haven't shown him anything, have you?"

Reina stopped so fast her tennis shoes kicked up tiny clouds of dust. "Where did you hear that name?"

"A...friend mentioned him," Emma said, crossing her fingers inside her pocket. "She, um, wants to introduce us."

"Don't do it." Reina's gaze turned serious and she put her hand on Emma's arm. "I've heard things about him. He's not what he seems."

Emma's pulse took a leap. "What do you mean?"

"There are rumors about him. Not good ones."

"Do you think he's—"

"I don't know what I think, only what I've heard, and he's someone to stay away from. He's not your kind, sweetie."

Reina might be the biggest gossip in town, but she never talked badly about people. "Have you met him?" Emma persisted.

"I've seen him. He came into our office, inquiring about renting a place. Another agent took care of him, but I saw him passing through. Later she told me who he was." Reina met Emma's gaze speculatively. "He's a very nice-looking man."

Emma nodded slowly. The smoldering, dark-eyed sensuality he possessed had struck her immediately, and she'd be a liar to disagree. And yes, she'd glanced in his direction more than once last night at the restaurant. Obviously she had more interest in him than she did in most of her clients. Not only had she e-mailed Leon about him, she'd now asked Reina about him. Still, it didn't mean she was interested in Raul Santos. At least not *that* way.

It was purely professional, Emma told herself. Nothing personal.

She turned the conversation in a different direction, and Reina seemed happy to oblige. They chatted until they finished the lap, then the two said goodbye, Reina driving off in her pride and joy— a Toyota Four Runner she'd paid a fortune for, given the exchange rate—and Emma trotting down the street. The park wasn't that far from where she lived, and she liked the extra warmup and cooldown time she got by walking there. Fifteen minutes later, she reached her street and then her house. Putting her key in the garden gate's lock, she turned it, then realized with surprise the gate was already open. She stopped and stared at the key ring.

She'd locked the gate when she left. She always did.

Despite the warm November sun, a chill of uneasiness swept over her. She quickly glanced up and down the sidewalk. The street was empty, and when she turned back to her house, it looked the same. Nothing appeared disturbed. The front door was shut, and the windows were tightly secured, just as they'd always been.

Should she go on in or...or what? You didn't call the police for things like this, not here. This wasn't the States. The guard at the bank did double duty sometimes, helping people with private security matters, but this hardly seemed worth bothering him about. And what if it was nothing? The man would say she was a fool, and before she could blink, everyone at the bank would hear the story. She couldn't afford anything remotely negative said about her at work.

She hesitated a moment longer, then resolutely pushed open the gate and stepped inside. Locking it securely behind her, Emma walked up the sidewalk to the entry. Her mouth suddenly dry, she reached for the doorknob and told herself she was being ridiculous. Everything was fine, and even if it wasn't, what could a thief take from her that mattered? Material things meant nothing to her now. All she really valued was her bank balance, and no one could get to that.

The old-fashioned knob was large and heavy. Emma twisted it sharply to the right, but it held and she gave a huge sigh of relief. She must have just forgotten the gate, that was all.

Unlocking the door quickly, she stepped inside. Her pulse continued to race, though, and just to be on the safe side, she called out, feeling silly all the same. "Hello? Is anyone here?" She switched to Spanish. *"La policía está aquí,"* she warned in a loud voice. *"Me entiende?"* The police are here. Do you understand me?

The only answer was silence, so she closed the door behind her. Listening closely, she stood immobile and waited. She heard no soft footfalls, no stealthy departure, no hint of anyone's presence. Finally, after a few more minutes of listening to her heart pound, she accepted what the stillness told her. She was alone.

Still spooked in spite of herself, she grabbed the wooden cane resting by the front door. She'd discovered it in one of the closets after moving in, and the heavy silver top, shaped like a bird's head, had kept her from throwing it away. She'd check out the house just to make sure. With the walking stick in hand, she went into every room. Nothing was disturbed or missing. By the time she made the tour—living room, dining room, kitchen, then upstairs into the two bedrooms and the bath—she'd convinced herself everything was fine. Of course, someone could have circled behind her to hide, but why would someone even be there? A thief would run.

She went back downstairs and into the kitchen, and that was when she realized she'd forgotten the maid's room. A tiny closet-size area with a separate bath, it had a door to the patio at the rear of the house. She gripped the handle of the cane and tiptoed to the closed door beside the refrigerator. Taking a deep breath, she twisted the handle and pushed open the door.

The room was empty. And the door leading outside was locked. Emma let out her breath in a *whoosh* and leaned against the wall, her legs suddenly trembling now that her foolish search was over.

There was no one inside the house. She was fine. She was safe. She'd simply left the gate unlocked, her mind on something else. Like Raul Santos.

She gave a shaky laugh and turned to go upstairs and shower. Just for good measure, she took the cane with her.

Over the running water, she never heard the back door close.

BY FRIDAY AFTERNOON, Emma was exhausted. The week had been a hard one, and she was looking forward to the end of it, despite the fact that on Saturday she had another party to go to. This one, a charity event, was out in the country at a club the expatriates favored called La Sierra. She didn't want to attend any more than she'd wanted to attend the last event, but business was business. Reina had told her William Kelman would be there, and that was all it took. He had yet to come into the bank. If Emma had to woo him some more to obtain his account, then she'd do it. She didn't have the luxury of being proud and hadn't in quite some time.

She spent the morning doing paperwork, her only interruption coming when her phone rang at close to one. She picked it up and answered.

"You have a call from the States," Felicity said. "A Mr. Leonard F. Davis III. Are you available?"

It took Emma a minute to recognize the name, but when she did, her throat went tight. "Put him through," she said.

The minute she said hello, Leon said excitedly, "This guy is something, Emma, the guy you asked me to look up. How'd you hook up with—"

She made her voice as businesslike as possible as she interrupted him and halted the flow of words. "Mr. Davis! What a surprise. I thought you were going to e-mail me this information." She glanced toward her open office door nervously. "I wasn't expecting you to call."

"I was gonna mail you, but when I saw this, I had to make it direct. I'm calling on my lunch break. I don't know what kind of bank you're working for now, but this guy's not like the customers we used to get here."

"What do you mean?" she asked calmly.

"Well, for one thing, he's into some serious money. Real serious. Most people don't carry six figures in their local checking accounts, right? Out there in El Paso, he's run more than that through on several occasions, some of it cash.''

Cash deposits of more than ten thousand dollars were always scrutinized. It meant tons of paperwork and hassle, but the banks complied; they had to or risk more than they wanted if the deposits were ever questioned.

''Did they check out?''

''All the forms were fine. Nothing fishy on the surface.''

As quietly as possible, Emma leaned forward in her chair, the phone in her hand. Felicity was at her desk, and as Emma watched, the secretary rose, picked up her coffee cup and walked across the reception area to the small kitchen that was concealed behind a screen.

''Could you find addresses for him?'' she asked quietly.

''Yeah, but...'' His voice trailed off. She could hear the sound of paper being shuffled, then he spoke again. ''There's something weird about it, though. He lived in Washington, just like you said, but there's a five-year gap.''

Emma waited for him to explain, but he said nothing more. ''A gap? What do you mean?''

''I mean a gap. The guy just disappeared for five years. He lived at 1019 Oak Cypress Drive for seven years, Unit 302C. Took the paper, subscribed to magazines, had a credit card, then everything stopped. It was like he flew to the moon or something. Five years later he resurfaced.''

''That's crazy. Are you sure you looked—''

''I checked everything. Nothing got past me, okay?''

Emma bit her tongue. She'd forgotten how defensive Leon was. ''And you did a great job, I'm sure. I just don't understand, that's all.'' She peered through her office door and caught Felicity going out into the hallway. She was heading for the main section of the bank, probably the offices out front. A new vice president had just been hired, and Emma had heard the secretaries giggling and talking about the man. Seeing the woman leave, Emma felt a moment's relief and spoke again.

''What do you think the gap means?''

''I don't know, unless…''

He didn't say more, so she pressed him. ''Unless what?''

''Well, he did live in Washington. Worked at a big law firm there—''

''He's an attorney?''

''Yeah, passed the bar first time he took it, no problem.'' His voice went up a notch. ''But listen, Em, maybe that was a cover, you know? Maybe he's one of the alphabet men.''

''Speak English,'' she said impatiently. ''What are saying?''

"He could be a spook. CIA or FBI. Maybe even DEA, since he was in El Paso, too."

She'd considered every possibility, but not this one. She was skeptical. "That seems a little far-fetched, Leon. And it wouldn't explain the money. Lawyers do okay, but not that well, and government employees certainly don't make that kind of money." *Except for William Kelman,* she thought unexpectedly.

"Maybe it wasn't from a payroll. Maybe he funneled it for someone."

She spoke again, this time almost to herself. "There's got to be another explanation. I can't buy this one."

"Oh, there's another one, all right, but you aren't gonna like it any better." Leon paused, the line falling silent for a few seconds before he spoke again. "The guy coulda been in prison. I checked but didn't find anything. That doesn't mean it didn't happen, though."

"Leon! That's ridiculous! What on earth would make you think—"

A knock sounded on her open door, interrupting her words. Emma jerked her head up.

Raul Santos stood in the doorway.

SHE ACTUALLY WENT pale when she saw him, Raul noted. With a quick mumble, Emma Toussaint hung up the phone and came out from behind her desk to greet him. Raul tried to read the emotion on her face as she walked toward him, but he wasn't fast enough. She recovered her composure immediately and placed a mask of politeness on her features. She'd been surprised to see him, but something more had passed over her face. Guilt? Confusion? Anxiety? He immediately thought of William Kelman and wondered if he'd been on the other end of the line.

"Mr. Santos!" she said. "How nice to see you. How are you?"

She held out her hand and he took her fingers in his, holding them as he answered, "It's Raul, remember? And I'm very well, thank you." After a moment longer than necessary, he released her hand, but the feel of her skin stayed with him. Soft and silky—and freezing cold. She was nervous.

He told himself she couldn't possibly have found out anything about him—not that fast. He smiled. "It was good to see you Monday evening. The restaurant is excellent, isn't it?"

"It is wonderful," she answered. "Did your friend enjoy it?"

"Yes, she did. I wanted to take her somewhere nice, but I had no idea where to go. She's the one who told me about Santa Cruz and the opportunities here." He held out the flowers he'd been holding by his side. "I brought your secretary a little

something to thank her for her help, and I thought
you might enjoy these, as well.''

The delicate fragrance of freesias and white
roses wafted up from the cone he handed across
the desk.

Her eyes widened in surprise, then filled with
pleasure as she brought the flowers to her nose and
inhaled deeply. ''How thoughtful of you! They're
gorgeous. Thank you very much.''

She looked both flustered and touched, as if it'd
been a long time since a man had brought her flowers. He murmured his reply, wondering what she
would think if she knew more about him.

He pointed to one of the chairs in front of her
desk. ''May I sit, or am I interrupting?''

''Please.'' She gestured toward the chair.
''Make yourself comfortable. Would you like some
coffee?''

''No, thank you. I've actually come to set up a
trade I'd like you to handle. You have that information I requested, don't you?''

Her expression went blank, then her brow fur-
rowed as she obviously remembered. ''Oh, my
God. I'm so sorry. Felicity told me you'd asked
for some stock reports and I completely forgot.
I've been so busy.'' She shook her head in an embarrassed fashion and abruptly laid the flowers on
her desk, turning quickly to the computer monitor
sitting nearby. She began to type as she talked, her

fingers flying over the keyboard. "Maybe I can get them on-line. If I put out a rush request, it's possible I'll have them by this afternoon..."

She wore a dark brown suit with a straight pointed collar. The severity of the cut and somberness of the color did everything it could to make her look unattractive.

But it failed.

He mentally shook himself and returned to the task at hand. The report didn't matter, but she didn't know that. It'd only been an excuse to return to the bank. He could use this opportunity to his advantage, though.

"You could make it up to me in another way."

Her fingers stopped abruptly, and she looked at him, her hazel eyes darkening. "How?" she asked cautiously.

"Have dinner with me Saturday. Surely by then the reports will be here, and we can discuss the details of the trade. You can execute it for me at the beginning of next week when you've got the time."

She wanted to say no. He could read the refusal on her face, but her business acumen wouldn't let her. He was a major client, and she didn't want to upset him. She couldn't *afford* to upset him. He felt a moment's sympathy for her, but ignored it and pressed his case. "It's the least you can do," he said with a smile, "to make up for forgetting about me."

"I didn't forget!" she said quickly. "I assure you, that's not the case. It's just that I've been busy and—"

"It's not important," he said, dismissing her excuse. "But come to dinner with me, anyway, and convince me of that."

She hesitated for a second. "I have an obligation that night, out at La Sierra—"

"Oh, yes, the charity auction for the hospital. Las Hermanas de Socorro. I forgot about it."

She was trapped, and they both knew it. If he'd been unaware of the event, she might have been able to get away with her excuse, but not now. He couldn't have worked it better if he'd planned it. He silently thanked Wendy for mentioning the gala.

"La Sierra is on the road to Cochibamba, isn't it?" he said in a pleasant voice. "I've heard it's quite lovely out there."

"It is." After a moment's hesitation, she spoke again, saying the only thing she could. "Would you like to go with me? I could introduce you to some of the other expats, show you around a bit..."

He looked into her eyes and smiled. "Tell me where you live and what time to pick you up."

BY SATURDAY EVENING, Emma had begun to ask herself just what she'd been thinking when she'd invited Raul to attend the party with her. Reina would see them and she'd give Emma a hard time later. William Kelman obviously had a problem with him, too. To top things off, Leon Davis had practically insisted the man was a felon. She'd known all this and she'd invited him, anyway.

As she pulled one of her endless black dresses from the closet, Emma tried to analyze what was going on, but she couldn't come up with an answer. Sure, she found him attractive, but she hardly knew him, for God's sake, and most probably shouldn't let it go any further. Since her divorce, she'd made it a policy never to date anyone associated with her work. Actually she never dated at all. It wasn't worth the effort, and besides, there were always questions, questions she didn't want to hear or answer. But now she'd broken all her rules and asked out Raul Santos. It didn't get any worse than that.

When he'd looked at her with those dark compelling eyes and handed over those freesias, she hadn't had a chance. Touched by his thoughtfulness, she had reminded herself that, in South America, it wasn't unusual for someone to show up with a small gift for no reason—a box of candy, a bouquet, a book. She'd received them before, so why the reaction?

Because she owed him, she told herself. She was embarrassed by her slipup with his account, and the truth was, he deserved an extra courtesy. If he wanted to go to a boring charity event with her, why not? Since asking him, she'd had more than one sleepless night to ponder the situation, but now, as it came down to the wire, she wondered if she was rationalizing her behavior.

Either way, the man would be on her doorstep in fifteen minutes, and she had to get dressed. She slipped off her robe and stepped into the black sheath, then her phone rang.

She picked up the receiver and Todd's voice sounded so clearly over the line he could have been in the next room. Her heart almost stopped. In all the time they'd been divorced, he'd never called. Not once. She immediately thought the worst.

"Todd! Is everything okay? Are the children—"

"They're fine." His words were clipped and businesslike, but his rich Louisiana accent was thick as ever beneath the coldness. To her, a poor kid from the bayou, his way of speaking had represented class and sophistication. He'd wooed her with that accent. She hadn't heard the cruelty in it until it was too late. "They're just fine," he repeated.

Relieved by his answer, she sat down on the edge of her bed, the mattress sagging. He spoke again. "That's not why I'm calling. I've got something else to tell you."

"All right." Her tone was wary. "What is it?"

"I'm getting married again. I thought you should know."

She had no love for this man, none whatsoever, but the knife he'd buried in her heart two years ago twisted once more. Now her children would have a new mother. They'd forget all about her. She opened her mouth, but no sound came out.

"Did you hear me, Emma Lou?"

He'd told her once that only poor people had two first names, and after they'd married, he'd refused to call her what everyone else did, shortening her name to Emma. Unless he wanted to make her feel like the miserable girl from the wrong side of the tracks whom he'd mistakenly married.

"I heard you," she said quietly.

"The proper response to the groom is 'Congratulations.'"

His correction was so typical she couldn't stop herself. "I think 'My condolences' might be more appropriate—at least for the new bride."

He made a sound of disgust. "Always with the smart answer, huh? My mother was right when she said breeding was everything."

Emma closed her eyes for a moment, then opened them again as she spoke. If she agitated him, the conversation would only get worse. "Who is she, Todd?"

"You don't know her." His words held as much disdain as ever. "She's a Threadgill from Charleston. Her people go way back."

"Do the children like her?"

"The children adore her." He took the handle of the knife and pushed it deeper into her heart. "They're already calling her mama, and they can't wait for the wedding. Sarah's going to be the flower girl and Jake's carrying the ring. We're getting him a tux."

"How...wonderful." She felt faint.

"I thought you should know what was going on," he said. "In case the kids said something when you called on Sunday. They're both excited about it, and I didn't want it to be a shock or anything to you."

She lay down on the bed, the phone still at her ear. "I understand."

"This won't change the custody situation," he warned. "Don't even think about calling the judge."

"I wouldn't dream of it." She told the truth; the judge had been in the family's pocket for a hundred years. Until she found a lawyer more powerful than any of them, the judge would never rule against the Toussaints.

"All right, then. Just so everything's clear." He

paused, his cruel work done, his drawl now more pronounced. "You doin' all right down there, Emma Lou? How's business at your bank?"

He didn't give a damn about her business, and both of them knew it. In fact, he'd done all he could to keep her from finding a job, period. Bolivia had been her last resort. He was gloating.

Emma ignored his question. She couldn't hang up without hearing about her children, though. She'd talk to them tomorrow, but she couldn't be this close without hearing more. She hated herself for doing it, but she begged, anyway. "Tell me about the children, Todd. Please."

She'd been a good girl, she knew, so he softened. She could picture him leaning back in his chair and swiveling it to look out the window of his study. She knew that was what he'd done, because she could hear the chair groan, then squeak. She knew what he was looking at, too. The backyard with the pool and the swing and the magnolia trees so perfectly trimmed.

His voice turned expansive. "Sarah's been givin' us hell this week. She's definitely in the terrible twos and goin' on to the intolerable threes. She tried to paint a picture for my mother, which would have been okay, but she used Sparky for a brush and a wall for the canvas. Took Nana three days to get the place repainted, and the damned dog still has a pink tail. Can't even take him huntin'.''

"And Jake?"

"He had soccer tryouts this week. Did great. Loves the academy, but I guess you know all 'bout that.''

Her son had had his first day of school in September, and the Sunday before he'd gone had been one of the hardest calls for Emma to get through. He'd been so excited. She'd had to hide her tears.

"How did his math test go?"

"He got an A." Todd paused, then, "He still likes his reading best, though. His teacher called me Monday and said she'd had to fuss at him for readin' in class and not payin' attention. Seems like he always has his nose in a book—just like you used to.''

Emma couldn't reply. Her throat had closed. For just one heartbeat, she let the pure feeling of misery engulf her, then she fought it. She wouldn't give Todd the satisfaction of knowing how deeply his words ripped into her. "That's good to hear," she said thickly. "I'm glad he's enjoying his schoolwork. He doesn't always tell me much about it.''

"Yeah, well…" Todd said. "You take care now, and the children will be talkin' to you tomorrow.''

She stayed on the bed for another few seconds

with the phone still in her hand and the line buzzing in her ear. She hoped the connection was still there. The wasted long-distance time would cost Todd at least some of his precious dollars and the adorable Miss Threadgill—she had to be adorable, of course—some future earnings, as well.

Finally, after a few more minutes, there was nothing else for Emma to do but get up and go on. That was how she existed, day by day, hour by hour. She put her past behind her and continued, the feel of her children's bodies when she hugged them, the sweet smell of their skin and the touch of their lips against her cheek only a memory. She hung up the phone, rose to her feet and slipped on her shoes, then walked woodenly toward the hallway and started down the stairs.

CHAPTER FIVE

RAUL OPENED the door of his black SUV, helped Emma climb in, then closed the door behind her. She'd greeted him at her front door, purse and jacket in hand, ready to go. He'd hoped for an invitation to step inside, but she hadn't offered one.

Quiet and somber, she obviously had something on her mind, and like always, he assumed the worst. William Kelman. Had the man already approached her? Raul wanted to ask, but she wasn't likely to tell him the truth at this point. She didn't know him well enough. Yet. Whatever was bothering her, she seemed determined to put it behind her as soon as they reached the road leading out of town.

"Do you know this highway?" she asked.

He shook his head. "I haven't been here long enough to know any of them."

"Then you're in for a treat. This isn't like anything you've seen in the States."

Before long, he understood what she meant. It was Saturday evening, and the route was packed—mainly buses filled to the top with people and animals, but a few cars and motorbikes puttered along, too. The shoulders of the roadway told the real story, though. Every hundred yards or so, there were animals hobbled and staked out, mainly cattle, but some goats, as well. Fences were too expensive, Emma explained, so the farmers kept their livestock where everyone could see. This marked their property lines and kept the well-tended animals in hand.

The huts on the side of the road didn't share the cattle's apparent prosperity. Made of mud bricks and thatched roofs, most of the houses had no electricity or running water, and there were very few vehicles in sight. One or two had carts tied up in front, but for those at the very bottom, even a cart was unaffordable. Raul had to stop the SUV at one point to allow a man, pulling a pig on a rope, to trudge across the road.

The farther out of town they drove, the less populated the area became. Bamboo plants began to replace the simple dwellings, and everywhere he looked, Raul saw green, in particular orange and lemon trees, their fruit-laden limbs bent to the ground. Even the air had a junglelike smell. They were going up, he realized, gaining elevation as they left the valley behind.

"It's a beautiful country, isn't it?"

Emma's voice sounded almost wistful. He glanced at her. "It is nice," he agreed, "but not the kind of place I would expect to meet someone like you.''

''Why not?'' Her voice held surprise.

''For one thing, you're too smart,'' he said bluntly, ''and for another thing, you're too ambitious.''

''How do you know I'm either of those things?''

''Easy. You wouldn't be at the level you are in the bank if you weren't ambitious, and if you weren't smart…you wouldn't be that ambitious.''

He continued speaking when she didn't seem to know how to reply. ''So explain how you got here,'' he said, softening his voice. ''There must be a story there, right?''

She stiffened visibly, her fingers tightening on the armrest. ''You really don't want to hear it,'' she answered.

''It doesn't take much to entertain me. Go ahead.''

She sat quietly for a few minutes and he wondered how much she would tell him. ''I came here from New Orleans,'' she said finally, ''after a nasty divorce.''

''It must have been pretty bad to make you come this far.''

''It was.''

He waited for more, but none came. He decided to push her. ''Do you have any kids?''

"No," she lied, looking out the window away from him. "No children."

Her deception surprised him, even though he should have expected it. "Just as well," he said lightly. "Less to worry about, right?"

She turned to face him. Her skin glowed in the filtered light of the jungle around them. "So you have no children?"

He shook his head, putting aside the dreams he'd had before as if they'd meant nothing. "No. No kids, no ex-wife, no ex-anything. I'm free as they come."

"You sound as if you like it that way."

He slowed to avoid a goat crossing the road. "It's all I've ever known. I guess I must."

They said nothing more until he saw the club's sign ahead. Slowing the truck, he pulled into the drive and eased over a grassy area that served as a parking lot. Expensive vehicles filled the space, all of them new and shiny. In a country where few could afford their own transportation, the excess stood out.

Automatically Raul began to search the grounds with his eyes, even before he and Emma reached the club's door. He saw no sign of Kelman, but there was plenty else to see. Under the trees, to the right of the doorway, was a huge cage, at least twenty feet high and fifty feet long. All Raul could see in it were blurs of frantic movement. Emma explained as she saw his puzzlement.

"That's where the monkeys live. The owner of the club loves animals. Everywhere you go, you'll see something, so watch out." She raised her eyebrows in a mock warning and smiled. "Especially for the parrots. They like to swoop in and take a bite off your plate when you aren't looking."

Again he had the thought that she looked different when she smiled. Younger, more carefree. The contrast of this to her eyes, where a deep sadness stayed, made her even more intriguing.

Raul shut down the part of his brain that responded to her pull. "Thanks for the tip. I'll be careful."

They entered the club under a walkway of thatched material, the heavy vegetation close and humid. From the fronds of the nearby palms to the brilliant plumage of the raucous parrots, the jungle seemed to close around them. Raul almost expected to see a wildcat or an anaconda as they walked into the main area of the club. A huge open room, the place was packed with expensively dressed men and women. They were all holding drinks and talking. Looking over the crowd, Raul decided his expectations had indeed been met. They wore the same predatory look as the jungle animals. Emma waded into the crowd with determination, and Raul followed.

They'd been there an hour when Raul saw him.

With a sense of déjà vu, he watched as Kelman worked the room on the opposite side. Just as he had that first night at the Taminaca Bar, he was talking to everyone and acting friendly, but the man's eyes searched the crowd continually. Raul followed his gaze until it stopped. Once again, it landed on Emma. They'd made the circuit of the room together, Emma introducing him to everyone. When she'd stopped to talk business with someone, he'd stepped away to give them some privacy, wandering to the other side of the crush. Now, as he looked on, she walked through a set of French doors to a terrace. Raul felt a flare of satisfaction, but it was followed by hesitation. Everything was falling into place exactly as he'd imagined, except for one troublesome exception.

He hadn't counted on liking Emma Toussaint.

AROUND THE CORNER from the French doors, Emma walked to the nearest planter and dumped her glass of wine into it. She set the flute on the railing that edged the area, then turned around quickly, her dress brushing the yellow hibiscus blossoms.

She needed to go back inside and work the crowd, but the fresh air felt wonderful and she paused to breath it in. The crush of the crowd had been getting to her, or maybe, she thought belatedly, it wasn't the crowd, but someone in particular. Raul.

His questions in the car had not been unexpected, but the interest with which he'd asked them had been. Despite all she'd heard and suspected, Raul Santos appeared to be a thoughtful person. There was a patina of something hard and impenetrable on the surface, but underneath, she sensed a man who truly cared, a man who was actually interested in her as an individual. At least, his questions had reflected that.

They'd also delivered a fresh level of pain, coming on the heels of Todd's announcement. Most of the time she simply avoided the answer, but with Raul, she'd flat-out lied, told him she didn't even have children. She didn't want him getting any closer to her, and in her mind, anyone who knew her past knew her. At least she'd learned something about him in return. He didn't like children, and he didn't like entanglements.

Somewhat handy, she guessed, if you tended to disappear for five years at a time. The thought reminded her of Leon's wild guess that Raul had been in prison. He might be right, but somehow she couldn't reconcile that idea with the man she was getting to know. Did felons give money to beggars and donate large sums to hospitals? Reina had told her about Raul's check to the Sisters.

Emma looked out over the valley and shook her head. The contrast intrigued her, despite herself.

She started back inside, but as she neared the corner, a loud voice off to one side halted her progress. She told herself it was none of her business and continued on, then she recognized the cool timbre of Raul's voice as he responded to the other person. She tried to distinguish the words, but the mountain breeze snatched them away.

Her curiosity getting the better of her, Emma edged forward. All at once, she realized she didn't need to get any closer. She knew exactly who Raul was speaking to; the unmistakable pungency of cigar smoke drifted to her in a haze of blue.

Following the smoke came William Kelman's voice. It broke the night's quietness with undisguised anger. "Are you trying to tell me you don't—"

"I'm telling you you're wrong, my friend." In complete contrast to Kelman's agitation, Raul chuckled. To Emma, the deep sound came across as something other than amusement.

"I'm here for the same reasons you are," Raul went on. "To make my fortune. Nothing more. I had no idea you were here. Why would you think otherwise?"

Her surprise was quickly overtaken by confusion. They obviously knew each other, yet Kelman had asked her about Raul when they'd been having dinner. Still hidden, she moved a step closer.

"You're saying your being here is purely coincidental?" Kelman's voice remained uptight, angry.

"What else could it be?"

"You know exactly what else it could be, Santos. You followed me. You're on some damned revenge kick, aren't you?"

"Revenge kick?" Raul stopped, the puzzlement in his voice clearing as he spoke again. "Do you mean Denise? That's over and done with, Kelman. Besides, why would I want revenge? As I remember it, the woman left you for me. Isn't that what happened?"

Silence, tenser than the words they'd just exchanged, filled the sudden void, and Emma half expected to hear the sound of a fist against a jaw. Her mouth went dry, her throat closing. It seemed preposterous that the two men would travel so far to fight over a woman, but stranger things had happened.

Kelman spoke first. "You don't know what you're talking about," he growled.

"Then why don't you inform me? Tell me what really happened." The sudden coldness—and the quick change—in Raul's words sent a shiver through Emma. It would have been less frightening if he *had* hit Kelman. "Tell me what I've been missing all these years, Kelman. You do know I missed a few, don't you?''

Another pause, then Kelman said heatedly, ''I don't know what kind of sick game you're playing, Santos, but I don't want any part of it. I had nothing to do with your troubles. You brought them all on yourself. Now get the hell out of my way.'' The pitch of his voice suddenly changed, and too late Emma realized why. He was heading straight for the corner where she stood.

She had a split second to think about it, no more. With a bravery she didn't feel, Emma straightened her shoulders and took a single step forward.

And crashed into William Kelman's chest.

''OH, MY!''

''What the hell?''

As they collided, Emma and Kelman spoke at the same time, her voice apologetic, his still angry from the encounter with Raul.

''Mr. Kelman, I'm so sorry. I...I didn't see you. Please forgive my clumsiness.''

Emma's pretty words were exactly what Raul would have expected to hear, but her expression, as she glanced over at him, was something else entirely. She'd overheard their conversation, he realized, and was wondering just what was going on. He stepped out of the shadows where he'd been and moved to her side.

He touched her briefly, solicitously, on the elbow. "Are you all right?"

"Yes, yes…I'm fine." Glancing back to Kelman, she tilted her head. "I see you two have met."

Kelman shot an angry look in Raul's direction. "Yes, we have."

Raul spoke easily. "Mr. Kelman and I go back quite a way, Emma. We're old friends."

Emma looked at Kelman with a puzzled expression. Before she could say more, he smoothed a hand over the front of his jacket and inclined his head. "If you'll excuse me, I need to get back to the party."

Emma nodded and stepped aside as Kelman brushed past her and disappeared into the room behind them. When she turned back and looked at Raul, her eyes were filled with questions. "He asked me the other night if I knew you. I just assumed you were strangers. What on earth was that about?"

"Nothing," Raul said. "Absolutely nothing." Taking her elbow in his, he began to walk along the edge of the terrace. Sooner or later, Raul had expected a confrontation, and it didn't really bother him. Whatever Kelman's plans were, he wouldn't risk them to stop and send Raul on his way.

Raul hadn't been as prepared as he would have liked, though, and Emma's overhearing the exchange complicated things even more. He had to distract her and quickly.

Within minutes, he had her away from the noise and confusion of the party. They stopped on the lowest level of the stone terrace and looked out over the valley. It was almost dark, and the low-lying hills were slipping into the shadows. Without the benefit of light to mark the boundary, the jungle vista seemed endless.

Before he could even begin to distract her from her questions, she turned to him in the darkness. "How do you know Kelman?" she asked. "What's going on between you two?"

He thought about not answering, but that would only make her more suspicious. He had to tell her something. "We knew each other a long time ago," he answered carefully. "He's a former DEA agent. I was a attorney in Washington. It's basically a small town—our paths crossed on occasion."

She looked slightly startled at his revelation of Kelman's former job. "And you don't like him," she said.

"Am I that easy to read?"

"No, not at all." She shook her head and confessed what her expression had already betrayed. "I overheard your conversation—part of it—and your feelings were obvious."

He shrugged casually. ''We crossed swords over what men usually cross swords over.''

''A woman?''

''That's right.''

''Was it Wendy, the woman you were with the other night?''

He looked into her eyes with a steady expression. ''No'' was all he said.

Before she could probe any further, Raul turned the tables. ''I answered your question, now you answer my mine. What happened to you right before I came to get you tonight? You seemed upset.''

She reacted with a flinch of pain, then cleared the emotion from her face so quickly he could tell she'd done it a thousand times.

''C'mon,'' he said. ''Turnabout's fair play. I shared with you…''

She took a long time to answer, then the words came out reluctantly; she had no other choice. ''I had a call from the States,'' she said finally. ''It was my ex-husband. He's getting remarried.''

Raul didn't expect to have a reaction, but it came, anyway. A moment's disappointment, maybe, a curl of displeasure? He wasn't sure what to call it, but it didn't matter. Surely he didn't care if she was still in love with her ex. ''I'm sorry,'' he said in a neutral voice.

"There's nothing to be sorry about. Those things happen. People move on."

"I'm sorry the news hurt you," he found himself saying. "That's what I meant."

She looked up at him, her eyes full of shadows, the hazel edging into a deeper green color. He got the feeling his words surprised her, but maybe that was because they'd surprised him.

"We've been divorced for more than two years," she said. "I expected him to have found someone before now."

"Why would you think that?" Raul met her gaze, turning so that he faced her fully. "I'd think he'd have a hard time."

She frowned. "What do you mean?"

"You're a very beautiful woman," he answered before she could finish. "You'd be a hard act to follow."

"Thank you," she said simply. "That's a nice thing to say, but Todd didn't see it that way."

"Then he was a fool."

Her gaze skittered away from his, then back before she spoke again. "I have my flaws."

"We all do."

Suddenly the urge came over him to kiss her. Not a simple touch of the lips, either, but a deep kiss that would make them both forget why they were here and what they were doing. The feeling was totally unexpected and caught him by surprise.

Would her lips feel as soft as they looked? Would they taste as sweet as he imagined?

With no further thought, he reached toward her, his fingers drawing a line down her cheek. Her skin was soft and smooth, but before he could pull her nearer, she stepped backward and out of reach, her expression remote, her voice cool.

''I think it's time to go back inside.''

He wanted to disagree, but he couldn't.

She was right.

THEY RETURNED to the party, and Emma found herself glad to be back in the light and confusion. Being outside with Raul had made her even more nervous than being in the middle of the crowd, especially after she'd read the intention in his black eyes. He'd wanted to kiss her, and for just one second, she'd wanted him to. The realization shocked her, but when she thought about it some more, she understood. He'd listened to her and wanted to know more about her. He cared. The unexpected knowledge made her heart thump with something that felt way too much like longing.

When they stopped at the bar inside, Emma excused herself and made her way to the lounge. She had to have a bit of time alone or she'd never make it through the rest of the evening.

The quiet moment wasn't to be. Reina caught up with her just as she entered the powder room.

They'd already exchanged a quick hello, and Reina had managed to let Emma know she didn't approve of her date for the evening. Emma had tried to explain that it wasn't a date, but Reina hadn't bought the story.

"Are you leaving soon?" Reina asked.

"I hope so," Emma replied. "I've enjoyed this about as much as I can stand."

"Let me take you." Reina's dark eyes met Emma's. "I've got to go to your side of town, anyway, and we could talk on the way home—"

Emma interrupted her. "Reina, I can't abandon Raul. I know you don't like the man, but he is my guest. I have to ride back with him."

"No, you don't."

Emma stared at her curiously. "Are you that worried about this guy? Just because you heard some gossip?"

"I don't like the way he looks." She threw a glance around the room. "And..."

"And what?"

A group of women, chattering like the parrots overhead, interrupted them as they swooped past and entered the lounge behind them. Reina pulled Emma to the side, out of their hearing and away from the traffic. "I've heard more," she said mysteriously. "And I like it even less than what I heard before."

His compliments still ringing in her ears, his

touch under the moonlight still fresh in her mind, Emma asked slowly, "What did you hear?"

"I can't tell you right now. I don't want to risk being overheard, but it came from a reliable source. Very reliable."

Emma stared at her friend, then it clicked. "Did William Kelman tell you something?"

Reina's eyes widened. "How did you know it was him?"

Emma explained the confrontation she'd heard between the two men. "There's bad blood there," she said. "Tell me what he said. Tell me now."

"He said Santos is a crook, that's what he said!" Reina glanced over her shoulder. "But I don't want to say more right now. Not here. Just call me when you get home, okay?"

Feeling uneasy but having no other choice, Emma nodded unhappily. A moment later, as she reentered the open-air room, she spotted Raul. He was standing exactly where she'd left him, near the bar. With the crowd swirling around him in a tangle of noise and exuberance, he was all alone, and she studied his unguarded expression. Wearing expensively tailored clothes and holding a drink, he regarded the room with a certain amount of boredom. Behind the gaze, though, was a sharpness, a kind of on-guard attitude totally at odds with everyone else. He wasn't there to party, he was there to work. Just like her.

The knowledge startled her, but there was no mistaking it. She'd worn that same expression herself too many times. So what did he want? Why was he there? His conversation with Kelman was also puzzling. Something was going on there—he'd worked too hard to distract her, she realized now.

Without any warning, she suddenly remembered her unlocked gate. She had no idea why she'd linked the two thoughts, but it frightened her, frightened her almost as much as her growing attraction to Raul.

He must have felt her stare. Lifting his eyes to sweep the room, his gaze locked on hers a second later. Like a river current, the connection was swift and strong. It carried her away before she could begin to fight it.

AS SHE CROSSED the floor to where he waited, Emma looked more worried and upset than she had when he'd picked her up earlier that evening. Despite her expression, in the press of overdressed and over-made-up women, her natural beauty drew his gaze and he felt a corresponding pull of attraction.

He simply couldn't figure her out; she was a mass of contradictions and filled him with the same. What he knew about her past didn't jibe with the obviously smart and together woman approaching him now. And the feelings she produced in him were the exact opposite of the ones he needed if he was going to fulfill his goal. How could he let her get tangled up with Kelman when all he could think about was kissing her? Suddenly the crowd and the noise and the loud music were too much to bear.

"Are you ready to go?" As she neared him, he put his drink on the bar and tilted his head toward the crowded room. "This is too crazy, even for me."

She hesitated for a second, then spoke over the din. "You read my mind."

A few minutes later, they were outside. The sidewalk was barely visible in the moonlight, the bamboo leaning over it, the cries of the caged monkeys and wild parrots taking over from the raucous rock and roll still pounding—but now more faintly—from inside the club. A cluster of white and purple orchids quivered in a nearby planter, their fragrance heavy and sensual in the velvet night. Raul found himself wondering how he would feel if he was here for a different reason. If he and Emma were actually on a date and he had no ulterior motives. Once, in a different time and place, he had been the kind of man who appreciated a setting like this.

They reached his truck and Raul helped Emma into it. Moments later they were speeding down the highway. The colorful scenes they'd witnessed on the drive out were gone, swallowed by darkness. Light from a few homes glowed here and there, but for the most part, the road was black, the lack of electricity almost eerie. Raul glanced across the seat at Emma. She was facing the window, her eyes studying the night as if she could find the answers she needed.

Neither of them spoke, and as the empty miles slipped by, Raul couldn't help but wonder what she must have thought of the conversation she'd overheard between him and Kelman.

His hands tightened on the steering wheel. What exactly had Kelman expected Raul to say when he'd confronted him? *Hi, I'm here to shake the hand of the man who framed me and put me in prison for five years?*

His knuckles turning white in the darkness, Raul thought back to the woman who'd started it all. He'd had no idea who Denise was when they'd first met. The stunning brunette had come on to him in a bar, and he'd accepted what she'd offered, as would have any man. All he'd seen was a gorgeous woman. He'd had no idea she was living with anyone, much less with William Kelman. Sick of Kelman's underhanded ways and tired of his overblown ego, she'd used Raul as an excuse. Within days of their meeting in the bar, she'd moved out of Kelman's place and into a tiny apartment of her own.

Kelman was well-known in Washington. He was flashy and obvious, and everyone knew he was with the DEA. Raul's biggest mistake had been to start an affair with Denise, and it'd almost cost him his life. *That's what happens when you think with something other than your brain,* Raul told himself now.

Once William Kelman had found out what his lover had done, Raul's life had quickly gone down the drain. He'd come home from a trip to the Bahamas, climbed into his car at the airport and started home. Before he'd gone a block, the red and blue lights of a police cruiser were flashing behind him. He'd pulled over and within seconds, a dozen other cops and five guys in windbreakers with ''DEA'' emblazoned on the pockets were surrounding him. One man in particular he'd never forget. He'd stood in the center of the road and smirked at Raul, a plastic bag of something powdery and white in his beefy hand.

''And what might this be, Counselor?'' He'd pulled the bag from Raul's trunk, along with a .45. Neither had belonged to Raul and he'd had no idea where they'd come from. The man's expression was unlike anything Raul had ever seen before, either. It'd taken him five years to figure it out, but finally he'd understood. It'd been gleeful, because he was paying off the devil. The agent was dirty, and Kelman had known. To get Kelman off his back, the agent had agreed to stage the stop, including the planting of the drugs and weapon.

They'd handcuffed Raul and led him away. Two months later he was in a federal prison in Cumberland, Maryland. There was no parole at this level for drug violations. The half a kilo of cocaine and the gun had netted him a six-year sentence. The cocaine they'd "discovered" in his car later disappeared from the evidence room, but the sentence hadn't. For five years and two months he'd wondered what had happened, then Denise Murphy had visited him and told him the truth.

William Kelman had set them both up. She'd gotten out earlier only because they'd planted less in her apartment.

William Kelman had stolen five years of Raul's life, and now it was payback time. He would take what meant most to Kelman, and that was his money.

The SUV had actually been stopped for a second before Raul realized he'd parked the car in front of Emma's home without even being aware of it. She reached into her purse, removed her keys and looked over at him. Her face was in shadow. "Would you like to come in?" she asked.

With thoughts of Denise floating around in his head, Raul hesitated. He'd wanted an invitation

earlier, but now he realized it was out of character
for Emma to ask him in. Then she moved and he
saw her expression in the light of a nearby street
lamp. She looked lonely, lonely and sad. Seeing
that emotion on any other woman, he would have
headed the other way. Reading it on Emma's face,
he had only one answer.

"I'd like that very much."

CHAPTER SIX

As EMMA USHERED Raul into her living room, she realized too late that it looked exactly like what it was—a place for entertaining that was never used. The maid came every day to sweep and dust, but glancing around the tiny parlor, Emma suddenly felt embarrassed by the sterility. It held no photos, no mementos, nothing to indicate that she had lived there for two days, much less two years. For the first time since she'd come to Santa Cruz, she mentally compared her house to the home from which she'd been expelled. It had been a sanctuary where lemon-polished furniture rested on hand-made rag rugs, and oils of her children gleamed from their places on the walls. The image brought a lump to her throat.

Raul seemed to sense her discomfort. "Do you have a patio or garden where we can sit? The weather's too nice to ignore."

Grateful for his perception, Emma led him toward the back of the house. They had to pass through the kitchen, which was messy, but at least it looked as though someone lived here. Stepping

outside to the bricked patio, she held out her hand.
"How's this?"

He smiled in the darkness. "Perfect."

She made her way to the chairs and table that
perched on the edge of the patio. More hand-me-
downs from the previous tenants. She pulled out a
chair and Raul surveyed her yard. It was planted
with a riot of tropical plants, and the night air was
filled with their fragrance.

He stood for a moment in silence, then breathed
in deeply as she watched, tilting his head to take
in the stars overhead. It was the gesture of a man
who'd been inside too long, and Leon's words shot
into her head.

A moment later, Raul stepped to where she sat,
taking one of the chairs and moving it closer to
hers. Over the scent of the flowers, she caught a
suggestion of spice, an aftershave lotion, she realized a moment later. How long had it been since
she'd noticed anything like that?

All at once, she regretted her invitation. It'd
been crazy. Impulsive. Totally foreign to her usual
behavior. What had she been thinking?

He started to sit down, then stopped. "Damn! I
can't believe I forgot," he said, snapping his fingers. "I brought you a little something, but I left
it in the truck. I'll be right back."

Emma watched him disappear into the house
only to return a few minutes later. He held out a
bulky newspaper. "A friend came in last night

from the States. I asked him to pick this up for you.''

Mystified, Emma took the paper and unrolled it. She couldn't believe her eyes as she took in the banner at the top. ''*The Times Picayune!* Oh, my God, how great!''

''I thought you might enjoy it. News from home is always nice.''

She shook her head with delight. ''You don't know,'' she said. ''It's been months since I saw one and this is yesterday's, too!'' Impulsively she hugged him, then drew back quickly. ''Thank you very much. I'll read it from cover to cover!''

He looked pleased by her reaction, a slow smile spreading across his face. Something warm and unexpected rolled down her spine. Trying her best to ignore the feeling, Emma folded the paper carefully and put it to one side of the table.

He tapped the paper. ''Tell me about your home there…about yourself.''

''You know all there is to know,'' she said lightly. ''I'm divorced, I've lived here two years, I'm a banker. That's it.''

''That's not who you are,'' he said. ''It's what's happened to you and where you live, what you do for a living, but it's not *you*.''

When she didn't answer right away, he prompted her. ''Tell me what you do in your free time, what you like to read. How you became a banker.''

"You don't really want to know all that stuff, do you? It's terminally boring, believe me."

She couldn't really see him, but she sensed his movement as he leaned closer to her. "I wouldn't have asked if I didn't want to know."

His interest was too much. It felt incredible to have someone this intrigued by her, yet how could she answer? She stood up abruptly and moved away from the table toward one of the hibiscus plants. Plucking one of the blossoms, she knew she had to say something, but she didn't know what.

His voice floated to her on the humid night air. It was closer than she would have expected, and turning, she saw that he'd followed her to the edge of the patio.

"What are you so afraid of?" he asked quietly.

She swallowed hard. "What makes you think I'm afraid of something?"

"You avoid saying anything about yourself unless I insist, and every time I get close to you— one way or another—you run."

In the dim light of an overhead street lamp she saw him raise his hand. Dreamlike, it came toward her face, and with the back of one finger, he brushed her cheek, an echo of his touch earlier that evening. The caress was so soft she could barely feel it.

"If I didn't know better, I'd think you were frightened of me."

"That's ridiculous. Why on earth would you

frighten me?'' She sounded brave on the outside, but inside, she was trembling. Her skin tingled from the simple heated contact.

He leaned a little closer, and for one panicky second, she thought he was going to kiss her. And she didn't want to move away, either, she realized.

''Tell me more, Emma,'' he said softly. ''Tell me who you really are…''

Although she didn't know what she was going to say, she opened her mouth to answer him. But she never got the words out. A loud crash shattered the silence into a thousand pieces. From the sound of metal on metal, it was clearly a car wreck, followed by a screeching alarm. With a loud curse, Raul whirled, bounded over her fence and ran toward the street.

RUNNING INTO THE CENTER of the boulevard, Raul shut off the car alarm with his remote, barely giving his vehicle a second glance. Whatever had happened, it didn't matter. *Who* was the more important question. His eyes searched the road, first one way and then the other. He caught the barest glimpse of a set of taillights careering around the corner, but that was all. He cursed again. Had Kelman somehow followed him to Emma's? The man knew where she lived, but the thought of Kelman following them home, watching them together, left a bad taste in Raul's mouth.

Slowing to a walk, he looked across the street

at his truck. The driver's side door was caved in, a long slash of stripped paint evidence of the other vehicle's progress from the back of the parked SUV and then along the side. It seemed to be a warning: *I don't know what you're doing, but I know you're doing it. Next time you might be inside the car when this happens.*

This was Kelman's way. Aggressive and nasty, but indirect. Staring at the damaged vehicle, Raul wasn't really bothered by the destruction, because he knew the man too well. Kelman would do nothing to jeopardize whatever plans he had—he'd only wanted to send Raul a message.

He crossed the pavement and reached the truck the same time as Emma. She raised her hand to her mouth in dismay. "Oh, my God! I can't believe this!" She stared down the street. "Did you see who did it?"

"They were already gone when I got here." He shook his head. "It doesn't matter."

"What do you mean, it doesn't matter?" Her expression was horrified. "It'll cost a fortune to repair this. And take forever, too!"

"It's only a vehicle," he answered.

She looked at him with an incredulous expression, then blinked, his meaning becoming clear to her. Without saying a word, she gazed again at the bashed-in door and bit her bottom lip. When she spoke, her voice sounded shaky. "Come inside and we'll call the police."

"No, that's not necessary," he said. "I'll handle it."

"But you can't—"

"I'll take care of it, Emma." Her startled look made him realize too late that his tone was sharper than it needed to be. "It's just not worth the hassle."

"But it's the law," she said stiffly. "You have to report accidents in Bolivia, or things get really sticky for you later. Raul, you don't want to mess around with the police here—"

"You're right," he interrupted gently, "I don't. So let me deal with this for now, and I'll contact them…later."

"All right." Her words held all the reluctance of someone who followed the rules.

Not of someone who broke them.

"All right," she said again. "If that's really what you want to do."

"It is." Walking around to the passenger side of the SUV, he opened the door. It wasn't easy— the car's frame must have been bent—and the door protested with a metallic screech. Reaching inside, he stuck his keys in the ignition. The engine turned over instantly just as he'd thought it would. If the wheel was free, he'd be able to drive.

Standing up, he turned to Emma. "Not a very good ending to our evening, huh?"

She wore an expression of distress. "I'm really sorry about this. It's usually a very quiet street.

Nothing ever happens here—'' She broke off abruptly, her words stopping awkwardly.

Stepping closer to the sidewalk where she stood, Raul sensed she'd been going to say more, but at the last minute, had thought better of it. He waited to give her another chance, but she stayed silent.

"Has something else happened here lately?" he pushed.

She started shaking her head even before he finished speaking. "No, not that I know of..."

She was so clearly lying and so obviously shaken Raul reacted without thinking, one thought foremost in his mind. *What in hell has Kelman done to her already?* He reached over, tilting her chin up, so he could look into her eyes. "You could tell me, you know. It would be all right."

She looked so startled that Raul wondered just what in hell *he* was doing. She recovered before he could answer that. "Nothing's happened." Her voice was stronger, more determined. "Absolutely nothing."

His reaction made no sense at all, but a sudden sweep of protectiveness, then anger, came over Raul.

He recognized at once how ridiculous the emotions were. He was here to use Emma, just as Kelman was, but emotions were emotions. They came without reason.

Just like the craving to kiss her. He didn't even bother to fight it this time; he simply gave in, leaning toward her and brushing his lips over hers, telling himself it would be enough.

But it wasn't. Her mouth was as soft as it looked, and instead of satisfying him, the kiss only made him want more. More of them. More of her. More. He pulled back abruptly, met her gaze, then climbed into the damaged truck and drove off.

EMMA COULDN'T REMOVE Raul's kiss from her brain, in fact, with each passing day, the moment seemed to grow in importance and take even deeper root. It had been nothing, a mere brush of his lips against her own, but she wasn't able to erase the sensation, no matter how hard she tried. It wasn't the feeling as much as the gesture; the brief touch had held the promise of more, and she had to remind herself she didn't want it.

She had a goal and nothing could stand in its way, including a romantic entanglement. *Especially* a romantic entanglement with someone like Raul, she amended quickly. A relationship with a man that intense, that focused, would be like standing under a magnifying glass. They'd burn up from the heat they'd generate. She could tell that just from his kiss.

But the more she thought about him, the more confused she got, especially when she realized he'd never asked her about his trade. Had he merely wanted to go out with her? He'd called several times since then, inviting her for drinks or dinner, but each time she'd turned him down.

If she didn't know better, she might think he was trying to court her. He'd brought her flowers, sent her candy...and the thoughtfulness of the newspaper! Only someone who'd been away from home for a long time knew what that meant. It wasn't just a paper; it was a bridge to everything familiar, a little link to the stores and the politics and the things you took for granted when you saw them every day. She'd read every inch of it, including the ads.

That night, he'd even invaded her dreams. Finally, about six in the morning, she drifted off into something close to rest only to have the phone sound an hour later. She wanted to ignore the baleful ringing until she remembered it was Sunday and Todd's turn to call her. She snatched up the receiver quickly; missing the call would have been awful.

Jake's voice reached across the miles and immediately captured her. "Mommy? Is that you? You sound funny..."

Sitting up in bed, she pushed the hair out of her eyes. "It's me, sweetheart. I was asleep, that's all. Remember how I told you it's not the same time here as it is there? We don't have daylight saving time like you do—"

He was too excited to listen. "Mommy, guess what I'm getting?" Not waiting for an answer, he continued, "You'll never guess. Not in a gazillion years."

"Okay, then, tell me." She blinked and tried to wake up more. "What are you getting?"

"A pony!" His words rang together in a string. "Charlotte's gonna move in here after she and Daddy get married, and she's bringing all her horses and she said I could pick out one just for me. Not one too big or anything, but one for my very own. Isn't that neat? I'm gonna call him Ranger. What do you think?"

He stopped to draw a breath, and Emma spoke in the gap, her heart suddenly in her throat. "Are you going to take riding lessons, honey?"

"Charlotte's gonna teach me." His voice was puffed up with importance. "She tol' Daddy she wanted to spend time with me. I heard her tell him. She hugged me and she smells nice."

The rest of the conversation was more of the same. Charlotte this and Charlotte that. Even Sarah had mumbled something about "'Lette," her young tongue unable to get completely around the other woman's name. Hanging up the phone twenty minutes later, Emma spent the rest of Sunday in a fog of depression. She should have been happy that Charlotte was treating the children so well, she told herself, but instead, she was jealous. She wanted to be the one teaching Jake to ride. She wanted to be the one holding Sarah's hand when she toddled around the yard.

Sitting at her desk at home the next morning, unable to face the day, Emma picked up the phone, called Felicity and told her she'd be working from there.

But she accomplished nothing. Her thoughts tumbled around like clothes in a dryer, going from Raul, to her children and back to Raul.

The memory of the kiss occupied most of her thoughts, but the car accident troubled her, as well. Her unlocked gate was nothing compared to the damage to Raul's vehicle, yet to have them both happen so close together was unnerving. She'd wanted to mention the open gate to Raul, then at the last minute had decided not to. The incident was so minor she felt foolish even to be worried about it, much less mention it to him.

To top it off, there had been the fight between Kelman and Raul. What kind of woman would those two men have fought over? Emma had called Reina that evening and told her more about the conversation she'd overheard. For the first time in their friendship, they'd exchanged angry words, Reina insisting that Raul was someone Emma should avoid. They'd apologized to each other before hanging up, but the tension was still thick between them.

Emma held her head in her hands and stared out the window. The monkey who lived in the trees next door was scampering from one branch to another, screeching and screaming as he shook the limbs and sent the leaves trembling as if in a storm. The irritating sound echoed inside her head, and for a minute, Emma thought about howling, too. The phone beside her jangled, saving her from her thoughts.

"Emma, I need to talk to you about something." Christopher Evans spoke without a greeting, and behind her boss's voice, Emma heard a note of unusual urgency. Typically unflappable, he sounded as if he was trying much too hard not to be worried.

But he was failing.

She couldn't imagine what might have upset him, but she felt her stomach knot in response, a cramp of nervousness she couldn't ignore. "What's going on?"

"That account you opened a few weeks ago for Raul Santos. Have you checked the funding on it?"

"I had Felicity look at it on Friday. She talked to the bank in El Paso and they said everything was fine—or at least that's what she told me." Emma hesitated. "Why do you ask? Is there a problem?"

"A problem?" His voice rose slightly. "Oh, no, there's no problem. Unless you think not having any funds to cover the check presents a problem."

CHAPTER SEVEN

EMMA SWALLOWED, her throat suddenly tightening. "It hasn't gone through?"

"Not as of this morning. I got our list of potential problems when I came in, and it was at the top. There were no funds in that account as of Friday at 7 p.m. I think you'd better talk to Felicity and find out exactly what the other bank said. And then you'd better contact Mr. Santos." He stopped again, then spoke. "You haven't traded on that account yet, have you?"

"No." She hated to explain, but she didn't have a choice. "He came last week to execute a trade. I didn't have some information he'd requested, though, and he didn't want to do the deal until he had that packet."

"Well, you'd better thank your lucky stars it worked out that way. Otherwise this conversation might be going down a much different track."

Emma's stomach took a dive. "I understand."

"Then you'll take care of this." It wasn't a question.

"Absolutely. I'll handle it, Christopher. Immediately."

RAUL CLIMBED into the rented Range Rover and started the engine. His SUV was still in the repair shop and probably would be for the next six months. As often as accidents happened in Santa Cruz, he would have expected faster service; then again, this was South America. The parts had to be imported, and the skilled labor necessary to install them was scarce. He had to wait his turn. In the meantime, the Rover would actually work out better, he decided. Kelman would have no idea now what Raul was driving.

He made his way through the convoluted traffic circles to Las Palmas, the suburb where Kelman lived. He tried to concentrate, but his thoughts were on Emma more than they were on the traffic. Since the last time they'd been together, she'd turned down all his invitations, and his frustration was growing. How could he find out what Kelman was doing if Emma continued to avoid him? He cursed himself for the kiss he'd stolen; the taste of her lips still lingered and the smell of her perfume haunted him at night. It'd been a mistake, and a big one. Getting close to Emma—hell, being attracted to her as he was—definitely muddied the waters. He'd have to watch himself in the future.

The entrance to Kelman's subdivision came into

view, and Raul turned the big SUV left, his thoughts shifting back to where they should be. It'd been easy to find out about the mansion Kelman bought, because there were only two Realtors in town who handled expatriates. Prepared to go to them both, Raul had lucked out with the first one. The agent had bragged about the sale, even though it hadn't been hers. She'd been very helpful, in fact, even driving him past Kelman's house to show Raul what he could get for his money when he decided to buy, as he'd implied to her he would.

The subdivision wasn't huge, but the houses certainly were. Mostly stucco with pools and lush landscaping, the compounds were surrounded by towering brick fences that marked each property's perimeter. They kept out everyone and everything, including prying eyes.

Raul eased down the street until he was almost opposite Kelman's home. On the sidewalk just outside the wall sat a tiny shack. It housed a series of guards whose primary task seemed to be visiting the maid next door. The only break in the brick came where the driveway intersected the fence. A set of double gates, made of iron and highly ornate, led inside to a garage. Raul knew the layout of the house and yard.

He had been inside twice.

Driving by slowly, he glanced toward the guardhouse. The guard was inside. Asleep. Raul circled the block, then parked, along with a line of waiting mothers, in front of a nearby school. Kelman would be out sooner or later.

Within a very short time, a horn sounded inside the gates, and the guard jumped up to open them. A shiny green Jeep—without any scratches—slipped through them a second later. Raul let several cars by, then he pulled into the street and followed a safe distance behind the Jeep.

Twenty minutes later, both vehicles pulled up outside the Banco Nacional.

Raul watched as Kelman exited the Jeep and headed up the sidewalk. He walked with a purposeful stride and rudely brushed off the Quechua, who had the misfortune to approach him with her palm outstretched. The bright spring day sparkled as he entered the bank through the side door, the door that led directly to Emma's office.

EMMA'S HAND shook as she disconnected the line, then reached out to redial her own office number. Felicity answered after three rings.

Emma spoke quickly. "Felicity, when you called that bank in El Paso to check on the Santos account, what exactly did they say?"

The secretary answered in Spanish, and Emma interrupted her impatiently. "In English, Felicity, please!"

Ignoring Emma's request, the young woman

spoke a second time, still in Spanish. "You have a visitor, Ms. Toussaint," she said. "I'm telling you in Spanish because he's sitting right here. He's very unhappy that you are not in your office."

"Who is it?"

Instead of giving his name, the secretary described the man. She clearly didn't want to let him know she was talking about him. "He's older," she whispered, "with short gray hair. He looks... intense."

"Did he give you his card?"

"Sí."

"Is it William Kelman?"

"Sí, sí, exactamente."

Emma closed her eyes. God, why had he come in now? When she wasn't even there. When everything was going wrong. She wanted to cry that the timing was bad. On the other hand, if there *was* a problem with Raul's account, she had a feeling Kelman's dividend could more than make up for the difference.

Taking a deep breath, she spoke rapidly. "When we hang up, tell the gentleman I'll be there in fifteen minutes. Offer him coffee or wine or whatever he wants, but for God's sake don't let him out of there. Do you understand?"

"Sí, sí."

"Okay, now tell me about the bank in El Paso. In Spanish, please."

"I called them, and they said there were no funds in the account, that it often ran close. They expected a deposit by the end of the day." Her voice turned fearful. "Did I do something wrong?"

"You told me they said everything was fine." Emma spoke through clenched teeth.

"That's what they said." The girl sounded near tears. "They said it would be fine, so that's what I told you."

"In the future, I need the details. I need to know exactly what they say, all right? Not your interpretation."

Crestfallen, yet clearly relieved, Felicity answered, "Yes, ma'am. I understand."

"Good. Now please give Mr. Kelman the message, then I want you to call Raul Santos and tell him I need to speak with him. Set up a meeting at any time and place he wants, but make it today. If he asks, tell him I need to firm up some details about his trade." She paused. "I really need to talk to him, Felicity, so I don't care how he wants to arrange it. Just make sure I get to see him today. I have to."

A second later, Emma hung up the phone, then ran to her closet, tearing off the robe she had on and grabbing the first dress her hand fell on. In five minutes, she was flying down the stairs and in another ten, after a wild taxi ride, she was opening the door to her office.

William Kelman rose when he saw her, his blue eyes flicking over her in a silent appraisal.

"I'm sorry I wasn't here when you arrived." Trying to appear calmer than she was, Emma crossed the room and held out her hand, smiling. "I had no idea you were coming in."

"I didn't, either," he said. "But I've decided to open my account, and I want to do it now."

"Great." Emma tilted her head toward her inner office. "Come in and we'll get started."

She was dying to find out if Felicity had contacted Raul, but Emma didn't stop to ask the secretary. She led Kelman into her office and sat down behind her desk.

Before Emma could even catch her breath, Kelman lifted a black leather briefcase and placed it directly in the center of her desk. Popping it open, then turning it around, he revealed the contents. It was packed with bundled currency—one-hundred-dollar bills—and the case was full.

Dumbfounded, Emma sat in her chair and said nothing. She was accustomed to large deposits, but not in cash, and immediately she wondered if the money was legitimate. Anyone who transported more than ten thousand dollars in or out of the U.S. had to file a report with the customs service. A 4790—a Currency Monetary Instrument Report.

Unless Kelman had filed one, which somehow she doubted, he'd smuggled the money in.

Without saying a word, he reached down to the side of his chair and picked up a second case Emma hadn't noticed before. This one held a jumble of paper. Each piece had a different design on it. Ornate with spidery lines and official-looking print, she recognized them immediately. They were stock certificates.

The number of shares, printed on the front of each certificate, ranged from one hundred to one thousand, and she knew the companies that had issued them. Anyone would. They were blue chip all the way. With fingers she had to consciously steady, she picked one up, flipping it over to read the back. It had been endorsed and was perfectly negotiable. She let it flutter back into the case.

Millions. Many millions.

The bonus she'd make from this deposit would be enough to cover an attorney and start proceedings against Todd. Her children's voices rang in her head, the clear sweet sound so real she wanted to weep.

Emma raised her gaze to Kelman's face and prayed she looked more composed than she felt. "Is this your deposit?"

"Yes, it is." He met her look with an open expression. "And before you even ask, I can assure you this money is clean, Ms. Toussaint. There's not a thing wrong with it. I've traveled back and forth to this country for many years, and I've brought some cash with me each time I've entered. I declared this every time I left the States, and you can check on that, if you like. The CMIRs are on record.''

Emma nodded slowly as he spoke. ''Then I'm sure there's no problem. Deposits of foreign currency are perfectly legitimate in Bolivia. We'll apply it directly to the account, and it will be immediately accessible. My secretary will handle it and give you a receipt for the total.''

With a pounding heart, she reached for her phone to ring Felicity, but Kelman's hand snaked out and stopped her. Her eyes shot to his. His touch was as cold as his stare.

''We have something to discuss first.''

He released her and her heart took an extra beat as she moved her hand away from the phone. It was hard to resist the urge to rub the spot on her wrist where his touch still lingered.

''I'm not sure exactly what I'll be doing with these funds,'' he said slowly. ''I may not want to trade them right away.''

''That's fine.'' She spoke confidently, but inside a million questions assaulted her. William Kelman unsure of what he wanted to do? Men like him were never unsure, especially when it came to money. She didn't know where the conversation was going, but calmly knitting her fingers together on the top of her desk, she said, "We can put it in an holding account where it can be available to trade—"

"I don't want to deposit all of it that way." His blue eyes glowed in the late-morning sun streaming through her windows. "At least not at first."

His implication wasn't entirely clear, but she moved to reassure him, assuming the worst. "Mr. Kelman, our accounts are very secure. Impenetrable, in fact. No one can—"

"Security's not my concern." He shook his head. "I have something else in mind."

She sensed the trap a second too late and spoke without thinking. "And that would be?"

"It's my understanding the government committee meets very soon—the committee that reviews the rate for the *boliviano* against the dollar. On the day the rate is announced, I want to be holding the appropriate currency—dollars or *bolivianos*." He stopped, his words suspended between them.

Emma looked across the desk at him, holding her breath, and remembered their earlier conversation, the one at Candelabra where she'd explained currency trading. If the Bolivian government devalued its currency, everything was suddenly worth less. Except dollars. You would want to own them and plenty of them. But if the government raised the value of the *boliviano,* the reverse would happen; the *boliviano* would be more valuable than the dollar. Either way, if you knew the direction in advance, you could make money. A lot of it.

But you had to know which way to trade.

Was he proposing she tell him in advance? His voice held no clue, no hint, of his intentions. It was calm and level, even friendly. It matched his expression, and she wondered if she was being paranoid.

"I don't believe I understand," she answered slowly. "The rate isn't published in advance. No one knows what it will be."

"Yes, that's correct, but not technically accurate, now is it?" He smiled.

Her heart thumped wildly as she mentally completed what she thought he was saying: *The bank knows the rate in advance. And you work for the bank.*

"There's a lot of profit there, waiting to be realized." He was speaking in such a convivial manner now that the tightness inside her eased. Surely she was imagining things. Then he spoke again. "And you know how it works... If I make money, you make money..."

Their eyes met again, and without warning, the week after her divorce flashed into Emma's mind. She had stood in the middle of her rented apartment, a drink in one hand and a bottle of pills in the other. At that very moment, she'd wanted nothing as much as she'd wanted to end the pain. It wouldn't have been the right thing to do—she knew that now—but the feeling bombarding her at this very minute held the same kind of temptation.

All her problems could be solved in an instant. She'd have enough money to buy and sell Todd Toussaint to hell and back. Her kids could be hers once more. She could almost feel her arms around their bodies.

"What do you say?" Kelman patted the briefcases, sensing her hesitation. "Can we work a deal that would benefit us both?"

She wasn't sure of her answer until she opened her mouth and spoke. "I don't believe I can help you with something like that."

He didn't look surprised. He merely regarded her with his hooded blue gaze. After several seconds, he spoke. "I intend on doing a lot of trading with this money. I would think your bank—and your boss—might appreciate that fact. Perhaps you haven't given this opportunity as much thought as it deserves."

Did he emphasize the word *opportunity,* or was she the one giving it more significance? She couldn't tell.

"I'm sorry you feel that way."

"I'm sure you are," he answered. She watched

his expression turn thoughtful. "I'll tell you what, though. Why don't you put the cases in the vault for me? Keep them for a while and think about my offer." Reaching into his coat pocket, he pulled out a business card and dropped it on her desk. "Here's all the information from me that you need. You think about it a bit...then call me."

There was nothing else she could do but give him a receipt and watch him walk out the door. Stunned and confused, Emma dropped into her office chair, her thoughts swirling in her head with the force of a tornado. Should she talk to Chris? If she was wrong and she accused Kelman of something he wasn't doing, she could kiss his account—and probably her job—goodbye.

Before she could decide, Felicity stuck her head in the open office door and delivered her message in a breathless voice. "Mr. Santos will meet you tonight at nine. At Michelangelo's."

The secretary closed the door as Emma nodded blankly, her eyes going automatically to the two briefcases. She stared at them for a moment, then she reached for the middle drawer of her desk. Pulling it open, she gazed down at the photograph she kept hidden there.

Jake and Sarah looked back.

RAUL DIDN'T BOTHER to ask the young secretary what the problem was. When she reached him on his cell phone as he sat outside the bank, he simply agreed to see Emma later that evening. Then, putting the SUV into gear, he headed downtown to the American Consulate. Whatever was wrong, Wendy could fix it.

She met him in the parking lot and climbed into the Range Rover, pulling at the skirt of her business suit. "You're in trouble, aren't you? And where's your truck? Why are you driving this?"

"It's a long story and I don't have time to explain. But I need your help."

She answered dryly. "That's what I'm here for."

He ignored her tone. "I think there's a problem with the money. Emma had her secretary call me and set up an appointment. I have a feeling the account in El Paso is screwed up. I could call and fix it, but you can do it faster."

"There's no problem with that money." Her words were matter-of-fact and assured. "It's a slush fund and illegal as hell. There's always cash in it, more than anyone can keep track of. Our agents draw from it night and day, whenever they need it." She paused for a second. "I could get fired just for telling you about it, much less allowing you to actually use the money. Not to mention everything else I've done…"

"Well, you have told me, and it's too late to stop things now. I want you to call and find out what's wrong, so I'll know before I see Emma tonight.''

"I'm not getting any more involved in this, Raul. I was crazy to think it'd work.''

"You weren't crazy. You were trying to help me. Now I need more help. If it makes you feel better, this'll be the last thing I'll ask you to do.''

Without another word, he passed the mobile phone to her. She held it for a moment, then with a sigh, punched in a series of numbers. Expecting her to speak, he was surprised when she tapped in a few more numbers, listened, then handed the phone back to him.

"The account is fine,'' she said tightly. "An agent down on the border drained it unexpectedly, so your check didn't clear. The replacement money was slow getting there, but it'll be available for transfer later tonight. Twice what you need. Maybe three times. Your secret is safe. But I can't guarantee for how long.''

"It won't take forever. Kelman knows who I am and he's already made his first move. He'll start to put his plan into action soon.''

She shook her head. "You're making a big mistake, Raul. The guy screwed you, yeah, but this…this is gonna get you hurt.''

"He didn't just screw me.'' The words were cold and clipped. "He stole five years of my life, and then he took away my livelihood.''

"You're smart. Find something else you can—"

"It's not that simple."

"It could be."

"You don't understand," he said tightly. "It wasn't just the years and it wasn't just being disbarred."

"I *do* understand. I knew you before you went in, Raul. And I see you now." She leaned across the seat, closer to him. "You're a changed man. You don't care what happens as long as you get him, and that's not the Raul I used to know."

He stared out the windshield. On the street by the consulate parking lot was a tiny kiosk selling cold drinks and cigarettes. He watched the proprietor go to the side of the minuscule metal building, open a three-foot-high door and climb inside. He appeared a second later inside the opening, ready for business, as he sat down on a stool and looked patiently down the street.

Turning to Wendy, Raul spoke. "You're right. And that's why I can't let this guy keep doing what he does, Wendy. He uses people, then he throws them away. One way or the other, I'm going to destroy him. If I do get hurt in the process, that's not good, but that won't stop me."

"So you'll do whatever it takes to get the job done?" She stared at him and shook her head. "Tell me how that's different from what he does."

"I can't," he answered. "But he set the play in motion. All I'm going to do is finish it."

EMMA GAVE HERSELF plenty of time to get to Michelangelo's, but two streets away from her house and four miles from the Italian bar, an impromptu parade broke out, and her taxi got caught in the middle of it. With a mariachi band playing in front of them and a decorated pickup truck behind them, she and the hapless cabdriver could only inch forward with the rest of the revelers.

She was accustomed to these spontaneous displays of exuberance. Bolivians loved parades and they occurred frequently, some more thought out than others. A wedding, a birthday, any kind of holiday, and the streets filled with vehicles sporting crepe-paper flowers and hand-lettered signs. Music—as loud as possible—was de rigueur for each of these processions, and costumes were always welcomed, too. The brighter and more colorful, the better. As the marchers spilled over the sidewalks and swept up people in the cafés, everyone was encouraged to join. Emma looked at the window with dismay, but there was no way out. They were stuck.

She leaned against the cab's dusty upholstery and tried not to panic. She'd been trying all day not to panic, and so far, she was failing.

Every time she thought of William Kelman's

leather briefcases sitting in the now-darkened vault of the bank, she wanted to throw up. Had she read him correctly or not?

She wished once more she could ask Christopher, but the more she thought about it, the more she knew she couldn't. Already upset about Raul's money, he'd think she couldn't do her job. A fact she herself was starting to wonder about. She'd checked again just before leaving the office, and the funds still weren't there. She was on her own with this one. That was nothing new, but another roil of nausea hit her as she considered the impact. Just once, she thought, just once...couldn't it be easy?

The taxi lurched ten more feet, and by the time they reached the bar, an hour late, she was almost beside herself.

Pushing her way in, she was sure Raul must have left. She edged into the crowd, anyway, searching the low-lit room anxiously. Like all the bars in Santa Cruz at 10 p.m., this one was packed, a smog of smoke hanging over the heads of the drinkers, a deafening flood of noise pouring from several speakers hanging from the ceiling. Instead of the beautiful local music, played on flutes and drums, it was American rock. Her anxiety ratcheted up another notch.

She had just made her way to the center of the bar when she felt someone grab her elbow. Swing-

ing around in surprise, she found Raul. He wore
black slacks and a dark shirt, his skin a burnished
copper as he leaned close and spoke in her ear.
"Let's get out of here. We can't possibly talk with
all this going on."

His words were warm against her skin, and
something equally heated curled in her stomach.
Telling herself she was crazy, she nodded, and he
took her hand as they fought their way through the
crowd. Leading them to the front door, he pushed
it open and they tumbled outside, the humid night
air immediately surrounding them. He didn't release her fingers as she began to apologize.

"I'm so sorry I'm late, but the taxi got caught
in a parade. I didn't think we'd ever get here."

The street was shadowy and quiet, and after the
noise of the club, the silence felt as thick as the
darkness. She could see his eyes, though. They
were wary. Through the point of contact at their
hands, she felt a kind of humming energy, an almost electric tingle.

"It's not important." Under his voice's usual
smoothness, she heard the same tension she saw in
his gaze. Tilting his head, he indicated the street.
"Let's walk. You can tell me what's going on."

She hesitated. He was making her nervous, more
nervous than she was already, and suddenly she
wasn't sure that going anywhere with him was
such a good idea. She turned and studied his pro-

file, then in a flash of intuition, she realized what was going on. He already knew what she was about to say.

He *knew* there was no money in the account.

CHAPTER EIGHT

EMMA SEEMED perfectly at ease, her voice steady, her words well chosen as she began to explain the problem. If he hadn't been touching her, Raul would never have known how nervous she was. Through the fabric of her jacket, though, he could feel a distinct tautness, a dead giveaway to her true level of discomposure. Anxious and agitated, she was wound up as tightly as the watch on his wrist.

As tightly as he was.

With his visit to her office today, Kelman must have somehow brought the net closer; Raul read the signs when he looked at Emma. Dark circles of worry underneath her eyes. The frown etched into her forehead. The tension in every line of her face.

"I know it's a simple mix-up with the account, and I hate to even bring it to your attention." Speaking calmly, almost apologetically, she continued, "We have to figure out what's going on, though. I'm sure we can rectify the problem with a phone call." Obviously feeling his gaze, she said,

"Do you have any idea what the problem might be?"

"No, I don't," he lied. "But I agree completely with you. I'm sure there's a simple explanation. In fact, I'd be willing to bet it's been cleared up and we don't even know it. Let's stop by your office and find out."

She looked nonplussed by his suggestion. "The branch in El Paso is closed now. It's too late to talk to anyone there."

"Are you telling me everything shuts down at night?" He laughed easily. "Come on, Emma. I know how the system works."

Her gaze turned cautious. "Funds *are* posted after hours," she conceded, "but I verified the account just before I left the office. The block was still there. It wouldn't have changed since then because—"

"It has," he interrupted confidently. "Believe me, it has."

She stopped on the sidewalk and slowly disentangled her hand from his. They were standing in front of a store, and the light from the window display was all the illumination he had. But he needed nothing else. She didn't believe him, and that much was very clear.

"I don't think you understand the depth of this problem," she said slowly. "Your bank in El Paso is refusing to pay on your check. They're saying there are no funds in that account. I think—''

"I know exactly what you think." He paused. "But you're wrong."

They stared at each other in the darkness. In the silence.

He took a step closer to her. In her expression he saw the need to increase the space between them, but she held herself still. He moved even nearer.

"You don't trust me at all, do you?" he asked softly.

"Trust has nothing to do with this. It's business."

"Everything involves trust, Emma. It doesn't matter if it's between banker and client, parent and child...or two new lovers." He raised his hand and drew a finger down her throat. The skin beneath his touch was as silken and soft as it had been the last time he'd caressed her. "We all depend on trust. Our instincts are made out of it, and yours are telling you to run right now. But you'd be wrong if you did."

She stood frozen on the sidewalk, a look of confusion on her face that pulled at his sympathies, even as he told himself it shouldn't. Betting he'd made the right guess about Kelman's earlier visit, Raul steeled himself and baited the trap.

"I want to be your friend." His voice was a whisper in the darkness. "Couldn't you use one?"

Her eyes jerked to his.

Bingo, he thought.

"Wh-what do you mean?"

"You know what I mean."

"I don't think I do."

"I can help you, Emma."

"I don't know what you're talking about. I don't need any help."

She was going to make it difficult, and he wasn't surprised. "Let's go to your office," he answered. "I'll prove to you the money is there. And then we'll talk."

She wanted to say no to his suggestion. He could read her answer as clearly as he'd read her tension a moment before. She couldn't refuse him, though, and if she tried to, he would have to do something. And it wouldn't be something she'd like.

She looked into his eyes and interpreted the unspoken warning.

"All right," she said faintly. "Let's go."

THEY WALKED QUICKLY down the sidewalk until they came to Raul's rented SUV. The wind had picked up since they'd left the bar, and it raged around the corner, greedily snatching at Emma's skirt as she climbed inside. Straight off the Andean foothills, the gust was hot and gritty.

Still, the feeling it left wasn't nearly as searing as the lingering trace of Raul's hand on her skin. Her reaction to the simple caress far outweighed what it deserved, and she knew why. It was her *anticipation* of what might come next.

For God's sake, what on earth was she doing? Things were spinning out of control, and she was thinking about kissing— *No, tell the truth.* She was thinking about making love with a man who was practically a stranger, and a dangerous one at that. She should have been worried about the problem at the bank, but instead, the thoughts flooding her mind were purely sensual. The light on his skin, the look in his eyes, the heat in her body...

I want to be your friend, Emma.

There was no way he could know about Kelman's offer. Absolutely no way. If she'd ever needed a friend, though, it was now. She thought back to the argument she'd heard between the two men. The fight had been over a woman, but there could have been more to it than Raul had told her. If he really knew Kelman, knew the kind of man he was, Raul could help her. She wouldn't have to do this all by herself.... The idea was so tempting she turned to study him, to see if she could somehow read the truth she sought so badly in his expression.

The headlights of a passing car illuminated his profile as she stared. His cheekbone was a blade, high and prominent, his jaw a dark shadow with a midnight stubble. Above his brow, a single lock of thick black hair fell heavily across his forehead. She wanted to touch him, to lay her fingers on his face and feel its roughness and contours. She could almost imagine the strength there, the energy, the intensity. Abruptly she forced herself to look the other way. She was acting insane, absolutely nuts. This man was not the kind she needed anywhere in her life, much less in her bed.

They reached the bank a few minutes later, and with the wind building to a crescendo around them, they hurried from the truck to the porte cochere beside her office. The angry drafts whipped against her as she found her keys in the bottom of her purse. With trembling fingers, she finally managed to unlock the door.

They were swallowed instantly by darkness and a tomblike silence.

"I need to catch the alarm." Emma shook out her hair, the strands tangled and twisted from the wind's touch. "Wait here."

He nodded as she walked quickly to a closet on the other side of Felicity's desk. The panel to the security system was hidden inside. Opening the door, she punched the number into the keypad. The code was a personal one, and in the morning, Christopher would know she'd been in. He teased her a lot when she worked odd hours; he'd think nothing of seeing her name on the printout.

By the time she finished and stepped out of the closet, the bank's security guard was at the door that separated the main lobby from hers. She crossed to the window set in the center of the mahogany panel. "Everything's fine, Jorge," she said. "It's just me."

Through the beveled glass, the older man looked sleepy, and unhappy that she'd disturbed his rest. Adjusting his uniform, he ambled off, back to the chair where he spent his nights. Security here was not what it would have been in the States. At home, depending on the bank, she might not have even been allowed to come in like this, especially with a client at her side.

Unlocking the inner door to her office, Emma crossed the marble floor and switched on the desk lamp. She turned to call Raul only to find him already there; he'd slipped inside behind her, a silent shadow.

In a matter of minutes she had her computer booted up and had logged on to the bank's database. Opening the center drawer of her desk, she consulted a small notebook and figured out the daily code. She tapped it in and looked up at Raul as the system processed the numbers.

"I'm very doubtful that anything has changed."

"I understand."

The screen in front of her flickered, the terminal bright in the otherwise dark office. Typing quickly, she opened the file that recorded money transfers, and at the bottom of the screen, a new figure had been posted. Surprise rippled over her in an unexpected wave.

"It's there, isn't it?"

She raised her gaze to his. "Yes, it is."

"I told you to trust me." Rising from the chair, he walked slowly around her desk to look down at the screen. She started to stop him, then realized it didn't matter. It *was* his account. If he wanted to see the numbers, he could.

He leaned over her shoulder and began to trail his finger over the monitor as he followed the figures. She stopped breathing at his closeness, but she reacted too late. His aftershave reached her, the same one she'd smelled earlier. Her stomach tightened at the masculine fragrance, and she tried to concentrate on something else. Her eyes went to his right hand as it rested on the screen. One of his knuckles on his ring finger was misshapen. It'd obviously been broken and never set years before.

"What happened to your finger?" The words slipped out before she could hold them back.

He glanced at her, then at his hand, his gaze switching back to her as he spoke. "I had a summer job one year in a canning plant. I caught my high-school ring on a piece of machinery. It kept going and my finger didn't. My dad popped it back in place, but I never saw a doctor and it healed like that.''

"A cannery sounds like a dangerous place for a teenager to work.''

"It was. But where I came from, a job was a job and I felt lucky to have it. My parents were migrant workers along the border between Mexico and Texas. We went from town to town and they picked vegetables for a living. My steady job was a real step up.''

"And now you have this." Emma tilted her head to the terminal. "You've come a long way.''

"Yes, I have," he said. He waited a moment, then leaned back and stared at her. "How far have *you* come?''

He'd asked about her past before, and she'd avoided the question. Now, in the darkened office with the wind howling outside, she was too exhausted and drained to think up another lie. Even more importantly, though, something was happening between them. Something that was drawing them closer and closer. She had fought the sensation as long as she could. But no more.

"Not *that* far," she said, glancing at the screen. "I grew up in Louisiana in a little place called Kenner. My parents divorced when I was just a kid, and I never saw my dad again. My mom raised me.''

"And sent you to LSU, where you earned a degree." He raised his eyes to her diploma hanging on the wall.

"I got a scholarship, or it would never have happened. I majored in finance."

"Then you got married..."

She nodded slowly and stayed quiet. What was there to say about that that mattered?

He went on, "...and then you divorced."

She nodded again.

He waited a few seconds. "But you didn't have any children," he said finally. Quietly. "So that photograph you're hiding in your desk drawer means nothing to you. The one of that beautiful little girl, and the boy who looks exactly like you."

Catching her breath, Emma followed his gaze. In the corner of the drawer the picture of her children seemed to glow. With accusation.

"Are they yours?"

She waited two heartbeats, then nodded. "Yes," she whispered. "They're mine."

The silence that built felt like a living thing, breathing and waiting between them.

"Why did you lie to me the other night?" he finally asked.

"I don't know." She swallowed hard, then shook her head slowly. "Yes, I do. It's because I don't have them. They live with their father, and sometimes it's just too hard to...to talk about them.''

She waited for the next painful question, the one that always hurt the most. *Why does he have them and not you?*

When it didn't come, she answered, anyway, something compelling her to speak—the same thing that was drawing them closer, she suspected. ''The divorce was...ugly. There were accusations made. Against me. He got full custody.''

''Did you fight him?''

''As much as I could.'' Her low voice contained regret, but not the oceans of it she usually carried around, the horrible, heavy burden that she never put down. ''His family is very powerful in Louisiana, and money isn't a problem. Until I can afford an attorney who isn't afraid of them, the things Todd said about me won't go away.'' She dropped her gaze and stared at her babies' faces.

''What did he say?''

When she didn't answer, Raul lifted her chin with one finger.

She spoke, knowing he'd never relent until he knew the truth. ''He told everyone who would listen that I was a dreadful mother and a horrible person.'' A cramp seized her heart. She had to wait for it to pass before she could speak again. ''The judge believed him and I lost all right to see my children.''

"He must have had a reason to do something that drastic."

She looked up into the black well of his eyes. "He did," she said hoarsely. "I was addicted to pain pills and alcohol."

The confession hung in the stillness between them. Raul's expression didn't change, didn't move. She couldn't tell what he was thinking.

"I...I had a car accident right after Sarah was born. It was a really bad accident, and I injured my back severely. The pain just wouldn't go away. I couldn't pick her up, I couldn't nurse her, I couldn't do anything. And poor Jake got ignored completely. I *was* a bad mother. When the doctor gave me something that made the pain a little easier to bear, I was ecstatic. It let me take care of the children again, be the kind of mother I wanted to be. My only complaint was that it didn't last long enough. I had a drink one night because I was so depressed about it all, and I realized the alcohol worked *with* the pills. It made the pain stay away longer."

"A bad combination."

"The worst," she agreed. "Before I knew what was happening, I couldn't function on my own. And then...I couldn't function at all. It was just what Todd needed. He'd wanted the divorce, anyway, and was looking for a reason. When we'd met, he'd thought I was someone he could manipulate and control, but I wasn't. I had a mind of my own and ambitions of my own, and he didn't want that in a wife.'' She shook her head and tightened her mouth. ''Actually, he hadn't wanted a wife, he'd wanted a trophy, and he fell in love with my looks, not me. I was a pretty blonde and seemed to be everything he wished for, but on the inside I wasn't the sweet little woman he'd thought. My problems gave him all the ammunition he needed. In one fell swoop, I lost my job, my children, my home and my husband.''

Emma stopped as a gust of wind rattled the windows and pulled her gaze to them. She caught her breath. The Indian woman was outside on the sidewalk, trudging forward into the steady blast as if it didn't exist. On her back, wrapped in the *aguayo,* she carried her child.

Raul followed Emma's gaze. Together they watched the woman until she disappeared around the corner. For a moment they were quiet, then Emma spoke again, her eyes still on the window.

''Our relationship had already fallen by the wayside, and the house never mattered. I didn't give a damn about any of it except my kids. They were my life. They *are* my life. And I'm going to get them back,'' she said. ''If it's the last thing I do on this earth, I'm going to get my children back.''

SHE LOOKED UP at him with defiant eyes as she made her pronouncement. There was so much pain

in her expression—and so much determination—
Raul felt a chill sweep over him.

Without another word, she turned to face her
computer again and tapped the keys rapidly, shutting it down. The hard drive whirred as it responded to her commands, then the terminal
blinked into darkness.

She rose in one fluid movement. "I guess I owe
you an apology," she said. "Obviously our system
didn't catch the deposit when it should have. I'm
sorry for the trouble."

Telling him her history had taken its toll. The
shadows beneath her eyes were darker than they'd
been when he'd first spotted her at the bar. She
looked wrung out, vulnerable—and more beautiful
than he would have thought possible.

It made him feel like the complete and utter bastard he was.

The upside was obvious, though. If she trusted
him enough to tell him this, then maybe she'd trust
him enough to tell him when Kelman made his
move. It was the perfect setup, Raul thought regretfully. Kelman himself couldn't have dreamed
a better scenario.

Emma started around the corner of her desk, and
Raul reached out a hand to stop her. She'd removed her jacket when they'd entered the office,

and beneath his fingers, under the silk sleeve of her blouse, he could feel her tense.

He met her questioning look. ''Thank you.''

''For what?''

''For telling me the truth.''

Without taking his hand from her arm, he moved around the edge of the desk to stand closer to her. The glow from the lamp made her blond hair gleam. Her skin looked as pale and luminescent as the light itself. Just like the first time he'd seen her, the only color in her face came from her mouth. Her lips were full and red.

''You know why you finally told me, don't you?'' He didn't wait for her answer. ''I do. It's simple.''

She smiled regretfully. ''Nothing in life is simple.''

''This is.'' He waited a moment, then continued, ''You trust me now.''

She didn't say anything, but he could see her thinking. If she denied his statement, their business relationship might suffer. If she agreed, she gave away even more of herself. It was a classic dilemma, and all she could do was acknowledge it.

''You're very clever, aren't you?''

He lifted his hands to her face and cradled it gently. The air was still and expectant around them, a complete contrast to the howling gusts outside. ''No, I don't think so,'' he said slowly. ''If I were clever, I wouldn't do this." He leaned over and pressed his mouth to hers. This time in a real kiss. A kiss neither of them could ignore when it was over.

She resisted for a heartbeat, then she gave in, her mouth melding to his. Her luscious lips were soft and forgiving. She tasted sweet, too, and for some unexplained reason, he flashed back to his very first kiss. Martina Garcia. Behind the bleachers when they'd both been in the sixth grade. He'd kissed a lot of women since Martina, but none of them had rekindled that initial flash of heat and pure desire. Until now.

After a moment, Emma's hands pushed gently at his chest, and he pulled back reluctantly. She stared into his eyes. "You're right," she said quietly. "That wasn't a very smart thing to do. But I'm glad you did."

RAUL PARKED directly in front of her house. Feeling too conflicted even to think about the consequences of what she was doing, Emma led him up the sidewalk to her gate, then through it, to the door. Her thoughts whirled, but she hardly noticed. Her body was the only thing that counted right now. Every emotion, every sensation, every feeling was something she'd never experienced before. The wind on her face, the heat of the evening, even the call of the wild parrots from next door—it all felt so different, almost unreal.

Raul's kiss had triggered something needy in her, something she didn't even realize had been missing until this very moment. As they entered her house and he swept her into his arms, she wondered blindly if it had been his kiss or his offer of friendship that had brought them to this point.

She had to have both, she realized now, and maybe he did, too. She wanted a man who needed her, but she needed a man who wanted her. There was a hidden side to him that called out to her, a side that said he'd been hurt, too. They could heal each other, at least for a night.

He lifted his hand to her face, cradling her cheek in his palm. Their eyes met and locked, then he lowered his head and began to kiss her.

CHAPTER NINE

SHE ENTERED his embrace with an urgency that surprised him, and he took full advantage of her passion, ignoring the voices in the back of his head that insisted he leave while he still could. Their advice was useless and he knew it.

He couldn't have stopped kissing Emma any more than he could have stopped his heart from beating. She was too soft, too tender, too willing to let his lips and hands put aside the pain that was now a part of her very soul. As his mouth covered hers and he tasted the sweetness of her tongue, he thought of the way she'd looked when she'd told him about her children. He had never seen that kind of anguish on anyone's face. It had ripped into him with a sharpness he'd never forget. In his past, he'd lost years, but she'd forfeited something even more precious. Her future.

Their kiss deepened and he knew he was lost. Lost and crazy, for sure. Raul wanted Kelman, and he'd counted on using Emma to get him. The way he felt about her this very minute was not part of the plan, and it never had been.

She murmured into his open mouth and made a sound of longing. Splaying his hands across her back, he answered her with a groan of his own, everything else fleeing his mind. A second later, he picked her up and began to climb the stairs to the second floor. To her bedroom.

She clung to him with her arms around his neck, and when they reached the top, she nodded to the right. He turned that way and entered the room that faced the street, the one where he'd seen the light and billowing curtains that first time he'd sat outside her house. A huge four-poster bed took up one wall, and he headed straight for it.

In two quick steps, they were there. Emma slid from his arms as quietly as a whisper, then raised her hands to his shirt. Unbuttoning it, she stayed silent, but behind her touch was a desperation that needed no words to be communicated. Raul felt the same way. He urged her out of her jacket and her skirt and blouse quickly followed. Within seconds they were both naked.

He said nothing; he was afraid to break the spell as he stared at her in the darkness. Like Emma's touch, he let his eyes communicate his thoughts. *You're beautiful. Beyond anything I ever imagined, even in my dreams.* Her gaze met his in understanding, then she lowered it and brought her pale hands up to rest on his chest. The feel of her fingers filled him with desire.

He forced himself to stand still and simply drink in the beauty of her body. In the dim light coming through the bedroom draperies, she was a carved statue, her skin the color of pearls. He knew at that moment he'd never forget, no matter what happened in the future, the way she looked right now. Her blond hair, hanging to her shoulders, echoed the creamy tint; the nipples of her breasts were a pale rose. The only shadow of darkness fell at the apex of her legs, and even there, he saw simply a deeper shade of ivory. She looked fragile and vulnerable, and staring at her, Raul felt as though he had just learned a secret no one else could possibly know.

Finally he could stand it no longer. He lifted his arms and put them around her, and the feel of her skin against his own ignited their passion immediately. They fell onto the bed, a tumble of arms and legs and open mouths. Emma's hands danced over his body, sending him into a spiral of passion. He returned the favor, his own touch sweeping over her and finding nothing but the soft neediness of a woman too long without someone who cared.

They kissed deeply, almost as if they couldn't part, Raul's hands slipping over her polished back to her buttocks. Cupping their sweet curve, he managed to bring her even closer. A moment later, he tore his mouth from hers only to drop it lower, then lower still, his tongue finding all the places she'd kept hidden until now. She moaned under his caresses, then arched her back and cried out.

When he rose above her, their gazes met in the gloom. Her lips were swollen, her eyelids half-shut, heavy with desire that had already been spent and that yet to be released. Without thinking further, he kissed her once more, her scent rising between them to cast a magical spell. For what seemed like a lifetime, they stayed that way, their lips their world, then finally he drew back once more. He reached for the foil-wrapped condom he'd brought with him. A second later, he entered her.

EMMA'S FIRST LOVER had been an older man, a professor at her college. She'd been young and ignorant, too naive to understand what was happening until it was over. Afterward, they'd continued, because they'd started and neither seemed to know how to end it gracefully. The second man she'd made love with had been her husband. Their time in bed had produced the two most precious people in the world—her children. If Todd's touch had been hurried, his kisses cursory, it hadn't mattered.

Neither of those two experiences meant anything anymore. Not after Raul's lovemaking.

Emma curled up on her side, the sheet pulled over her bare breasts, and stared at the closed door of the bathroom. The sound of running water escaped from beneath the threshold, a shadow accompanying the noise as Raul apparently crossed the room. She shut her eyes for just a second and ran her fingers over her mouth and down her neck. Her body felt the same, but how could it be? Surely it had changed under the fire of his touch, welded itself somehow into another form altogether. It must have, for she felt completely different on the inside.

She lay perfectly still and relived the past hour. She felt as though she was in shock. Nothing had prepared her for this…this complete annihilation of her previous experiences. It wasn't just the fact that Raul had touched her, she realized slowly, it was *how* he'd touched her. His fingers going over her skin as if he were a blind man, his lips covering her mouth as if he was dying of a thirst only she could quench. Raul had devoted himself to her, and in doing so, he'd lifted her up to a place she'd never been before. She truly felt *loved*.

She opened her eyes slowly and rolled on to her back, her stare going to the ceiling. She knew the truth and she wasn't trying to fool herself; Raul didn't really love her, and she didn't love him. They had come together in the heat of passion and nothing more. She was a fool to think there might be a possibility for something else. She didn't even *want* it to be more, she told herself. There was no place in her life for love, other than that for her children. All her energies had to go in that direction. Yet, for just a moment—

She abruptly cut the thought off. He didn't love her, but there was something there, something that made her desperately want to tell him about Kelman. But what could she say? She wasn't even sure that the man was trying to bribe her. And what if he was? Handling the problem was no one's responsibility but her own. She shook her head, her hair whispering against the pillowcase. She was losing it. Sleeping with a client was bad enough; talking about another one with her lover was even worse. She draped an arm over her eyes as if to blot out her thoughts with her vision. A moment later, she felt the mattress move. She jerked her arm away to find Raul sitting on the edge of the bed, staring at her. She hadn't even heard him return.

From the open bathroom door, a thin shaft of light fell on part of his face, illuminating his cheekbone and the line of his jaw. The rest of his face remained in shadow. Emma looked at him and thought about what she'd done, how she'd let this man into her life—into her bed—even though he was almost a complete mystery to her. She'd only seen a sliver—like the pale yellow beam—and she knew nothing of the rest.

He seemed to sense what she'd been thinking. "Regrets?" he asked.

"No." She answered quickly—and truthfully—despite her thoughts.

"Good." He leaned down and kissed her. Pulling back slightly, he raised one hand and plucked a lock of her hair from the pillow to rub between his fingers. "You're a beautiful woman, Emma. Inside and out. I'd hate it if you felt this was a mistake."

"That only happens when one person expects more than the other can give," she said. "That's not the case here."

He looked at her in confusion. "What do you mean?"

She rose to support herself on her elbows. "We aren't in love," she said bluntly. "This means no more than it needs to—for either of us."

He leaned closer to her, his black eyes inches from her own. "Are you a mind reader?" he asked. "How do you know what it means to me?"

His words threw her off, confused her. "I...I'm just making things clear," she stammered. "I know you aren't looking for a long-term relationship. And I understand that. I'm not, either. I just wanted to let you know that was okay."

"But what if I was?"

"It doesn't matter," she said. "You aren't."

Their eyes locked. "You don't know that for sure," he persisted. "You don't know what I'm looking for."

She tugged the sheet higher, suddenly cold. "You've never been married. Never had children. You told me yourself you liked it that way. I assumed you meant it."

He shrugged. "You're right," he said carelessly. "But things can change. Just because a situation is one way right now doesn't mean it'll always be that way." He turned, the light now gleaming on his shoulder. "Things can change. *People* can change."

His words were curious, but to press him would be useless. She could tell that just by looking at the stiffness of his back. She'd touched a nerve, and she knew exactly how painful that could be. Raising her hand, she traced a pattern down his back, her fingers smoothing the ridge of his spine.

"What kind of lawyer were you back in Washington?" she asked quietly.

"I practiced family law."

Nothing could have surprised her more. "Family law?" she repeated. "You mean, like divorce... and custody battles? That sort of thing?"

He nodded. "I worked for a big law firm. The cases were heartbreaking. It wasn't work I enjoyed, but I usually felt as if I was doing some good."

"Why did you leave?"

"It was time," he said cryptically. Turning to face her once again, he leaned down and kissed

her before she could ask anything else. And within
a few seconds, she didn't care that he said no more.

TUESDAY MORNING, when Emma crossed the
lobby to give Christopher the report on Raul's account, she again briefly considered telling him
about Kelman. Just as quickly she dismissed the
idea for several reasons. One, bosses hated problems—potential or otherwise—and telling Christopher about it now, after the fact, would do nothing but make him think she was second-guessing
herself. It'd make her look weak and inefficient.
She'd taken care of the problem and there was no
reason to tell him about it. Besides, the bank paid
her to handle her accounts, and that was what she'd
done. She'd handled it. Kelman might not think it
was over, but she knew otherwise.

As she approached Chris's office, she knew
there was another reason she didn't want to bring
up Kelman's name. It was going to be hard enough
to get through the meeting just talking about Raul.
She wasn't sure she could do it and not give away
what had happened between them. She had to,
though. There were no rules about sleeping with
clients, but Emma wanted nothing of her private
life to enter the realm of her professional one.

She knocked on the door to Chris's private area,
then opened the door.

Glancing up from the reports he'd been reading, Chris regarded Emma with a neutral expression.

She nodded toward his desk. "I see you got the news. The Santos account was funded last night."

"I looked at it first thing this morning." Tapping the file with his pen, he shook his head and sighed. In his fifties and balding, Christopher Evans did his job and did it well, but he was only passing time in Bolivia, just like everyone else. It wasn't a place he'd aimed for, but circumstances had brought him here.

"I checked the account last night," Emma said. "I certainly didn't expect to see the funds, but they were there when we came in."

"We?"

She licked her lips. "I asked Mr. Santos to meet me last night so we could discuss the problem. He was positive the funds had arrived and insisted we stop by and check." She held out her hands. "And he was right. They were there. Maybe there was a glitch in the system."

He looked skeptical. "A glitch? I don't think so."

"I don't, either," she confessed. "But the money was there when we looked. I imagine our draw beat his deposit—that's the only explanation."

"The main thing is, it's there now," Chris answered. "And it's a good account, Emma. Congratulations. You did well for the bank by landing it.''

The praise was unexpected, and Emma smiled, albeit nervously. ''Thanks. I was glad to get it. The money will certainly come in handy.''

''I'm sure it will.'' He paused. ''But stay on top of it. That's a pretty big balance. We don't want to get involved in something sticky. Things are different here, but we still have rules. Make sure he fills out an F-Bar.''

The F-Bar was a report of Foreign Bank and Financial Account, and Chris's reminder was purely routine. Any U.S. citizen holding more than ten thousand dollars in a foreign account had to file this report with the IRS. Hidden assets were something the feds didn't care for—they couldn't tax what they didn't know about. Yet Emma's pulse took an unexpected jump. If Chris felt he had to warn her about Raul's account, what would he say about Kelman's offer?

''I'll keep an eye on it,'' she answered thickly.

Making her way back to her office, Emma threw a glance at the vault as she passed by its stainless steel doors. Kelman's briefcases were locked inside, but she knew they were there, like a snake waiting to strike.

She'd made plans to have lunch with Reina, so she worked until a little past two, then headed out, stopping at Felicity's desk to explain where she was going. "I'll be back in an hour. If Mr. Kelman comes by, tell him I won't be gone long."

Standing in the shade of a tobaruchi tree, Emma waited for Reina. The Japanese restaurant they were going to was nearby, and it was just as easy to walk as it was to catch a cab. Emma felt her mind go right back to the night before. Thoughts of Kelman and Raul, but mainly Raul, took turns driving her crazy. She prayed she wouldn't slip and say anything to Reina. The other woman would go nuts if she knew what had happened. A minute later, Reina flew up the street, fanning herself and fluttering with apologies.

"I am so sorry." Reina linked her arm through Emma's and gave her a soulful look. "I had a client I just couldn't get rid of, or I would have been here on time, I swear it. You aren't mad at me, are you?"

With a start, Emma looked down at her watch. She hadn't even realized until Reina spoke that she'd been waiting fifteen minutes.

"Oh, my God!" Reina squealed. "You didn't even notice, did you? For once you would have thought I was on time, and I blew it."

"You're always late," Emma answered, hoping Reina wouldn't notice how flustered she was. "What does it matter?"

Crossing the street, they dodged a scruffy dog and two children chasing it. "It *doesn't* matter to me,'' Reina said with a sidelong glance. ''But it usually does to you.''

As they drew closer to the restaurant, the walkway became more crowded, and Emma acted as if she hadn't heard her friend's comment.

Reina had radar for Emma's feelings, though, and she wouldn't let the topic die. Pausing at the curb, they waited for a light, then started to cross a minute later. ''What's going on?'' Reina asked as the crowd pressed in around them. ''You're upset about something. I can tell.''

Before Emma could answer, she felt a bump from behind, then an unexpected push against her side. ''What the...'' She sputtered an expletive and stumbled slightly, grabbing her purse a little closer as she did so. After regaining her balance, she turned to look over her shoulder to see if she could spot the culprit. Only strangers with blank and unfamiliar faces looked back, yet for one quick second, she thought she saw a flash of gleaming dark hair and even darker eyes. Raul?

Reina jerked around even faster. She'd felt the push, too. ''¡Ten cuidado!'' she cried. Take care! Cursing soundly, she grabbed Emma's arm and bustled them to the other side of the boulevard. A few minutes later they made their way into the restaurant and collapsed on one of the padded cushions beside a low-legged table.

''These people!'' Reina shook her head and

gratefully accepted the cup of tea the waiter poured. "I can't believe it. They're incredibly rude. Are you okay?"

"It's nothing," Emma replied. And it was. She was actually quite relieved. The incident had taken Reina's attention away from her question.

They placed their orders for shrimp tempura and the fresh sushi they both enjoyed, then Reina turned her relentless gaze to Emma as the waiter left. "Now tell me what's wrong."

Emma should have realized Reina wouldn't let the topic go. She paused for a moment to gather her thoughts. Even if she could tell her friend everything, she wouldn't even know where to start. "I can't." She tried to soften her voice as she fibbed. "It's business. And I really can't discuss it."

"Business I can understand. I thought it might be Raul Santos."

Emma carefully reached for her teacup and took a sip. "Why would you think that?"

"Why? Gee, I don't know, Emma. Maybe because the last time we talked I told you to stay away from him and you haven't. And you've been avoiding me, too."

"That's not true! I've been swamped with this problem at work and—"

Reina stopped her explanation with a wave of

her hand. "But you had time to go out with him last night."

At Emma's startled expression, Reina nodded smugly. "I have friends besides you, and they hang out at places like Michelangelo's." She leaned closer. "Are you crazy? What are you doing with that man, ¿*chica?* William Kelman told me he's bad news."

Just hearing Kelman's name made Emma flinch. She tried to cover up. "And I told you I saw them fight. I hardly think Kelman's a reliable source on this one, Reina."

"Well, I think this is something you better verify," her friend shot back. "And fast, before you get in over your head."

Emma tensed and held her breath. "What do you mean?"

"Raul Santos just got out of prison, Emma. He was there for five years. For selling drugs."

CHAPTER TEN

RAUL HANDED the Indian woman two *bolivianos* and told her to keep the change. It was twice what the iced drink cost, and her eyes widened at his generosity. She did what he said, though, and hurried down the street, quickly pushing her cart ahead of her as if worried he might change his mind. He hardly paid her any attention as she rattled around a nearby corner. He was focused on the restaurant across the street. Emma and her friend had gone in there a few minutes earlier.

He'd left Emma's house—and her arms—early that morning. The wind had died during the night, and a heavy fog had moved in to replace it. As they'd stood on her porch, the mist had clung like diamonds to her hair.

He'd looked down into her heavy-lidded eyes and had one thought: What kind of son of a bitch was he? When she found out who he was and everything he'd done, she'd remember the way they'd made love—and she'd hate his guts. It wouldn't be important to her that for just a few hours she'd given him back his life, that for just a little while, she'd made him feel like the man he used to be. Someone a woman like her could love, someone who'd dreamed of a family of his own and a life shared with others.

She'd know nothing of that.

She'd know only betrayal.

He cursed softly and shook his head. It'd been done. There was nothing he could take back, and in truth, he had only one regret—that it was over. If he closed his eyes right now, he was sure he could still feel the satin of her skin against his hands and the scent of her body as it'd heated in his arms. Cursing again, he tightened his jaw and forced such thoughts to the back of his mind. He'd just seen something more important than what had happened last night. He needed to concentrate on it, instead.

A man had bumped into Emma right in the middle of the street. In and of itself, that was nothing. Everyone walked everywhere in Santa Cruz, and the sidewalks were often crowded. But this man was not a simple stranger.

For a reason he couldn't explain, Raul had left Emma's house and gone straight to Kelman's. The man who'd later stumbled into Emma had pulled out of the Las Palmas mansion driveway an hour after Raul had parked nearby. He'd driven directly to the bank and waited in the shade without moving until the minute Emma had left her office.

At that point, he'd gone into action. Following her closely, he'd moved in tighter and tighter until that moment in the boulevard. Raul wasn't sure what the game was, but he knew one thing—running into Emma had not been an accident. The guy had planned it from the very beginning.

And that meant Kelman had planned it from the very beginning.

Leaning against a nearby fence, Raul thought about Kelman's background. He knew all the old tricks, and he'd invented a few new ones, too.

Kelman had chosen Bolivia for the same reason everyone else who wanted to do something illegal did: it was an easy place to accomplish such tasks. Raul had found him without trouble. Denise had told him she thought Kelman would return here, and Wendy had confirmed his arrival.

Which brought Raul back to where he was. Kelman had obviously hired this man to follow Emma. To follow her, then bump into her in the middle of a crowded street. She'd been surprised and had grabbed her purse, turning at the same time to see who had shoved her. She'd almost caught sight of Raul, but he'd ducked behind a group of schoolgirls. She hadn't seen him, or if she had, it'd been such a quick glimpse she hadn't believed it was really him.

Swearing once more with frustration, Raul closed his eyes for a moment and let the scene replay itself. *Emma walking. The man behind her. The bump. She turns and grabs her purse, her expression confused.* He played it one more time, examining every detail.

A second later, his eyes flicked open and he understood.

"IN PRISON?" Emma's stomach dropped. She felt the jolt as it hit the floor beneath where she was sitting. "Are you sure?"

"Of course I'm sure. He was charged with possession of cocaine *and* he had a gun." Picking up a California roll with a delicate pair of chopsticks, Reina arched one eyebrow. "Do you think I'd make up something like that? Kelman told me."

Emma turned the information over in her mind. Sure, it was coming from Kelman, but hadn't Leon Davis suggested the very same thing? He hadn't found a criminal record, though, she argued with herself. She might be fooling herself, but she had to believe he was exactly who he said he was. It was the only way she could protect herself, even if it didn't make sense.

"Well, if it's true, what does it matter?" She spoke almost defiantly to Reina but avoided her eyes. "People who've been in prison have to have bank accounts, too, you know. What would you have me do? Tell the man to take his business elsewhere? You know I can't do that. I need every account I can get.''

Reina stilled. Her sushi, caught in the chopsticks, hovered over the tiny bowl of fiery wasabi on the table between them. ''If he's doing something illegal and you get involved with him, Chris could find out. It could mean your job, Emma.'' Her dark eyes filled with concern. ''What would you do if...''

Emma froze. She'd been on automatic pilot last night, her body taking control, her mind too confused for any thoughts like this to intrude. Her mouth went dry.

''Don't say it,'' Emma answered sharply. ''No one's going to lose her job, okay? Especially not me. It's too important.''

Reina nodded unhappily. She was one of the few people in Bolivia who knew Emma's story. ''I just want you to be careful,'' she said. ''That's all.''

Emma squeezed Reina's fingers. ''I will be, so don't worry about me.''

They finished eating with Emma turning the conversation in another direction. It was all she could do. Reina's news was too much to handle right now. Emma had to think about it on her own time, when things were quieter. One thought did intrude, though. If Raul had been in prison—and for drugs, at that—she wondered what he'd thought of her confession the night before.

"Are you still going with me on Saturday?" Emma asked as she reached for another roll.

"You bet. I'm putting together a box of clothing and some other household things, as well. The sisters still need them, don't they?"

"They always need things." Once a month Emma visited an orphanage in Samaipata. It was one of the first places she'd visited after she'd arrived in Bolivia. At the time, she hadn't understood her need to see the rows of bunk beds and small shoes all lined up in a row. She'd known only that the bank supported the nearby orphanage, and when Chris had asked her to take over the responsibility for getting their check to the sisters every month, she'd eagerly handled the task in person.

Now she knew why she did it. It was a penance. A way of dealing with what she'd had—and what she'd lost. Until she had the resources to recover her loss, she would be a mother who had no children. What she *could* do was visit the children who had no parents.

"They're having their festival, you know." Emma dabbed her mouth with her napkin. "A parade downtown and everything."

They worked out the details of the day trip, then paid their bill and left. The sidewalks were just as crowded as they had been before, and the two women found themselves fighting to get back. Finally they reached the bank.

Emma gave Reina a quick kiss. "So I'll see you on Saturday, right? Don't be too late. I'd like to get there before dark for a change."

Laughing, Reina nodded, then all at once, a shadow fell across the two of them. Emma looked up and saw Raul, poised at the bank's side door. He smiled and her heartbeat quickened in a way she couldn't ignore.

"Either you're going a long way or she's always late." His eyes took in Reina's face as he held out his hand. "Hello. I'm Raul Santos," he said. "I'm a friend of Emma's."

Reina's face held surprise for a moment, then she spoke. "I'm pleased to meet you." Allowing him to hold her hand a second longer than he needed, she turned on the South American charm. It practically oozed from her pores. "I'm always late," she said, her accent growing heavy. "It's too hot to be in a hurry."

"I agree completely." His gaze turned to Emma, and there was a secret message in his eyes. It told her he was remembering the time they'd spent together and planning on more. Her pulse thumped wildly. "So where are you going that you can't be late?"

"To Samaipata. There's an orphanage there that the bank helps support. We're going on Saturday."

"An orphanage? And you visit it often?"

"It's part of my job."

He met her eyes, and once again, he seemed to read in their depths what no one else could. "They're very lucky, then."

The passion from the night before apparently still lingered between them. She prayed Reina couldn't tell as she answered with a neutral voice, "Our funds go a long way to help the sisters run the home."

"I understand."

And he did. She could feel his compassion and sympathy reaching across the narrow space that separated them. It felt warm and good. Far too good.

"Perhaps I could join you." With a sideways glance, he brought Reina back into the conversation. "If you wouldn't mind, that is. And I'd make a donation."

Emma hesitated a second too long; Reina answered for them both. "It would be sizable, your contribution?"

He smiled at her. "With my banker involved? It would have to be, or I have a feeling I'd never be allowed to forget it." Reaching into the pocket of his suit, he immediately removed his checkbook and a gold fountain pen. When he ripped the check off and handed it to Emma, she saw it was more than generous. There was no way she could refuse it—and no way she could turn him down. Reina would go crazy.

He replaced the pen and leather wallet, then looked at Emma. ''Why don't I stop by your place and pick you both up on Saturday? Around nine?''

He'd trapped her. Again. She nodded her acquiescence and echoed his words faintly. ''At nine.''

As he left them and headed off down the sidewalk, Emma turned to Reina. ''I thought you didn't want me around him.''

''I was wrong,'' Reina answered darkly. She said nothing else. Emma looked up to follow her friend's gaze. Raul was weaving in and out of the passing crowd. Only after he was gone from sight did Reina speak again.

''When there's a snake like that in the garden, you best keep an eye on him.''

EMMA SPENT the remainder of the week agonizing over the coming weekend. She couldn't decide if she should confront Raul with Reina's news or simply ignore it. She'd called Leon Davis to get him to check his records again, but he wasn't there. The bank's secretary had told Emma he'd gone to Nepal for two weeks. Some kind of adventure vacation.

When Saturday dawned, Emma woke up more restless and anxious than she'd been all week. A strong urge suddenly came over her to call Jake and Sarah; she *had* to hear her children's voices even though it wasn't Sunday. Maybe Todd would relent and let her speak to them.

She quickly found her purse and began to dig anxiously, looking for her long-distance calling card. Her fingers came up with a receipt from a bookstore, a tube of lipstick and a piece of dried-out candy before she finally found the card. She snatched up the receiver and dialed the familiar number, then listened to the clicks and rumbles and various other sounds that always accompanied an overseas call. After a few seconds of static, the phone began to ring. It was answered immediately. Expecting Jake, since Todd never picked up that fast, Emma felt a quick smile spread across her face. Until she realized she didn't recognize the voice at the other end.

"Toussaint residence. May I help you?"

The voice held a Southern drawl. Not the soft, slurry Louisiana accent that belonged to Todd, but a more refined one, laced with steel. In a flash, Emma realized who the speaker had to be.

It was the perfect Miss Threadgill. Of the Charleston Threadgills.

For a single, idiotic second, Emma thought of hanging up. Of not saying a word and just slamming down the phone. But she couldn't. She had more class than that.

"This is Emma Toussaint," she said coolly. "I'd like to speak with my son, please."

There was a slight pause—a hellish pause—then the woman answered. Her voice was so polite and perfect Emma wanted to throttle her immediately.

"I'm sorry, but Jake isn't available at the moment."

"And why is that?" Emma made her own tone even and calm.

"He's occupied and can't be disturbed."

Emma gripped the edge of the windowsill. She was standing in her bedroom, but in her mind's eye, she saw her son. "He's seven years old. How 'occupied' can he possibly be?"

With the kind of aplomb that only comes from old money, the woman spoke again, ignoring Emma's question. "I don't believe it's the proper day for you to be calling, is it?" The cultured tones dropped. "Are you...confused?"

A flush of heat rushed up her neck and suffused Emma with all the anger she'd been holding in check. "I'm perfectly aware of what day it is." She spoke through gritted teeth. "I'm going out of town tomorrow, and I thought it might be possible to speak with my children today, instead. They are still mine, you know."

"You gave birth to them, yes."

A vein in Emma's temple began to throb. She could feel it. "What about Sarah?"

"She's still asleep."

"And Todd?"

"He's not here."

"Then put on Miss Pearl. I'll talk to her." A woman who'd ruled the Toussaints' kitchen forever, Miss Pearl had looked at Emma with pity when Todd had thrown her out. Her pity had stung, but at least she hadn't turned the other way. She'd tell Emma how the children were, if nothing else.

"Miss Pearl is no longer with the family. A chef from downtown has been hired."

Emma felt a scream build inside her chest, then all at once, she realized how utterly helpless she was, how hopeless the situation had become. This woman with the cool, measured voice held all the cards. If she wanted to, she could crush Emma and never look back.

Sitting down carefully on the chair beside her bed, Emma took a deep breath. She expelled it softly and spoke as calmly as she could. "All I want is to say hello to my son, and then I'll hang up and go away. That's the only thing I need from you." She waited a moment. "Please let me speak to him."

She expected the woman to rebuff her coldly, anticipated her refusal. But it didn't come. Only silence answered her plea. After a second that lasted forever, she finally spoke.

"All right," she said. "Just a moment and I'll get him."

Pure white joy rushed through Emma at the victory, then Jake's voice came on the line and she focused once more. She had no real idea what he was saying—it was a jumble of words and phrases about horses and school and a new computer game—but that didn't matter. Only the sound of his voice did. The high-pitched giggles, the little-boy nonsense, the relentless chatter. She soaked it up like a sponge. When he stopped to take a breath, she asked him about his baby sister. "She's fine," he answered. "We went to the movies last week and she got to pick, but next week Daddy said I could pick and then..."

He continued for another five minutes, then ran out of steam.

She hung up and cried for fifteen.

CHAPTER ELEVEN

WHEN RAUL DROVE UP to Emma's house, she was waiting for him outside. Her eyes were red-rimmed, and despite the makeup she'd used in an attempt to cover up the evidence, it was more than obvious she'd been crying.

He met her on the sidewalk and stepped inside her walled garden, pulling the gate shut behind him. "What's wrong?"

She started to shake her head in a motion of denial, then stopped. "I just had a telephone run-in with my husband's fiancée. She tried to keep me from talking to my son...and I let it get to me."

Raul wrapped his arms around her and held her tightly, a surge of rage running through him that someone had this kind of power over her. Emma's body felt frail and she was trembling, but underneath the sadness, he could tell there was anger, too.

Her tears came fast and hard like a summer storm. "I'm so...sorry..."

"There's nothing to be sorry about."

She continued crying, her head against his chest,

until the sobs finally began to ebb. After a moment, she looked up at him and he saw that her irises had darkened into a deep forest green. She stared back, clearly pulled by an invisible force that neither of them could deny, no matter how much they might want to—or need to.

They stood that way, apart yet together, then she shocked him. She deliberately raised her arms and linked them around his neck, drawing his head to hers. As soon as he was close enough, she began to kiss him. It was a kiss of need. She wanted him to obliterate the misery, to take away the pain of what she had just gone through, and she knew exactly what she was doing.

He obliged her without thinking twice.

She murmured his name into his open mouth as he smoothed his fingers down her back, then lower to the curve of her hip. Beneath his hands, her body was soft and giving, and a rush of desire coursed through him. As if she felt the same jolt, Emma moved even closer. He held her for as long as he dared, the kiss becoming more passionate as her breasts pressed into his chest, then he pulled back. He had to.

She looked up, her mouth slightly open, lips swollen.

"Maybe we should go inside," he said.

She nodded, turned and started up the walk. He followed, and a few seconds later they were inside.

He opened his arms to pull her to him, but at that very moment, somewhere in the house the phone rang.

Their eyes locked and held, then she backed away from him, her sandals whispering against the floor as she turned and crossed the hall. He leaned against the front door and took a deep breath.

He heard her murmuring voice rise slightly, as if in argument or disbelief, and he started forward in the direction she had taken, toward the back of the house. He found her in the kitchen, gripping the phone.

"How bad is it?" she asked with concern in her voice.

She listened to the answer, then seeing Raul's questioning expression, shook her head.

"I hate to hear that," she said after a moment. "But I understand. Stay in bed and take care of yourself."

She listened for another minute, then spoke. "I'll be fine," she said quietly. "Don't worry. No, no. It's okay."

She hung up. "That was Reina. She's sick, something she picked up from a client." She started to say something more, but instead, paused and shifted her stance to look out the kitchen window to the garden beyond. Clearly she was trying to make a decision, and Raul stood by silently. Finally she spoke again, her back to him.

"Maybe it'd be best for you to leave," she said. "This isn't important and we don't have to go."

He waited for a second, then made his own decision and crossed to where she stood. Placing his hands on her shoulders, Raul experienced again what he'd tried to stem outside, an emotion he didn't want.

He forced the feeling down, back into the box where it belonged. Turning Emma to face him, he looked into her uncertain eyes. "Let's go without Reina. I want to see Samaipata. And you need to take the bank's donation."

"I'm not sure..." Her words trailed off.

"If you don't show up, you'll disappoint the children."

She nodded slowly.

"It'll be okay."

She looked up at him then, and his unspoken message communicated itself through his touch and his gaze. She nodded again, and they left.

THE TRIP WENT BY fast. Raul was a good driver, and the Range Rover handled the horrible road as if it were the finest highway. They arrived at the orphanage in record time, which was good for Emma because she was an emotional wreck.

She'd thrown herself at him like some kind of desperate woman. She hadn't had any other choice; her need to feel some kind of love had swept through her like a tornado. As addictive as a drug, his embrace had felt too good, too safe, too wonderful to ignore. She'd never done that kind of thing before with any man, but Raul made her do a lot of things she hadn't done before. Like ignore her better judgment. Instead of kissing him, she should have been asking him about what Reina had told her. Deep down, though, Emma didn't want to ask, because she didn't want to know the answer. The consequences of Raul's having been in prison were something she couldn't deal with right now. Maybe later, but not now.

Emma was happy to see the main street of Samaipata. The tiny village was a madhouse— there were people everywhere preparing for the parade, laughing and hanging crepe-paper roses, calling out to each other and decorating windows with bright paint. Emma gave directions to Raul, and within a few minutes they were driving up to the compound.

"Park over there." She pointed toward a shaded area just outside the wall that surrounded the buildings. "We can get the kids to unload everything."

Raul nodded and eased the truck to the spot she indicated. Then, before he could even cut the engine, the gates flew open and a flock of children— all girls—spilled from the opening and ran toward them. Behind them came two nuns. Dressed in brown habits with hems that brushed the ground, the two women beamed and waved to Emma.

Emma introduced Raul to the nuns as they climbed from the truck. ''This is Sister Maria and Sister Abelia,'' she said. ''They work here with the children.''

Raul shook hands with the two women. Their fingers were rough and work-worn, and he could only imagine the tasks they accomplished every day just to keep the place running.

They greeted him in Spanish and a little broken English, then began to chatter with Emma. The children swirled around them like a cloud of un-bridled energy. Raul watched in awe, though Emma had already prepared him for what to ex-pect. The girls ranged in age from three to eigh-teen, and they all wore the same thing—white dresses with blue trim. There were 120 students in the parochial school, none of them boys.

Leaving the women to their talk, Raul unlocked the back of the truck and began to remove the boxes and place them into the children's waiting arms. It looked as though Emma had been collect-ing clothing and anything else she could lay her hands on for months. With everyone loaded down, the girls started into the compound. Raul handed Emma a smallish box, then took the largest one for himself. He had to stop and watch, though, as she headed for the buildings. Her progress was slow.

With every step, more children greeted her. Little girls and big, hanging on her, touching her, kissing her, so starved for attention they clung as closely as they could. Over her shoulder, she threw him an apologetic look, but then she focused solely on the children. The cool, remote banker was replaced by the woman he'd suspected was underneath, the one he'd glimpsed earlier in the day—a vulnerable, caring individual who had a lot of love and no one to give it to. The pain of seeing these kids must have been overwhelming, yet she had time for them all. There wasn't a single child she didn't touch or kiss or somehow connect with. It was amazing.

She was amazing.

"Is this a government facility?" Raul finally caught up with her and glanced around as they passed through the gate. The barren courtyard wasn't exactly homey, and the square concrete buildings were stark and ugly in the hot sunshine. In the dirt two chickens scratched.

"Not exactly." A pair of parrots swooped and screeched in a nearby cage as Emma dodged three dogs chasing a fly. "The government is supposed to give them fifty cents a day per child, but they never do. The place is funded by private donations—from churches in Italy and America mainly. Which makes sense."

One of the younger girls grinned up at Emma

and murmured something. Emma bent down and gave the child a quick kiss, then raised her eyes to see Raul staring at her.

"Why is that?" he asked.

"It's usually Americans or Italians who come here for the children. No one in Bolivia adopts."

Raul stopped on the sidewalk. "What do you mean—Bolivians don't adopt?"

Emma halted, too. "They don't accept the children as their own. It's a cultural thing."

"Then all these kids will end up in America?"

"No. Not these." She shook her head slowly and met his eyes. "No one from outside Bolivia can adopt a child older than five. It's the law. But they won't take them themselves. Most of these kids will never have parents."

IF SHE'D HAD any doubts about what kind of man Raul was, Emma lost them at the orphanage.

She took him through the entire place. Through the dormitories, where each room had six small beds each with a stuffed animal sitting on top of them. Through the cafeteria, where the tables were already set for the next meal. Through the laundry room, where two washing machines worked twenty-four hours a day. Through the garden, which produced far too little for so many.

The children were shy around Raul at first, but the longer he and Emma stayed, the bolder the little girls became. Finally he gave in, picked one up and carried the lucky child in his arms as they'd toured the outer buildings. All of three years old, if that, she grinned and flirted, batting her eyelashes at him, then finally put her head on his shoulder in blissful delight, her eyes dragging shut. He carried her up to her room and laid her down on her cot. Tenderly. Quietly.

Watching with a tight throat and a sting behind her eyes, Emma had almost broken down and wept. She could easily imagine him doing this with a child of his own, a little boy who looked just like him, or a little girl as dark and gorgeous as the one he'd just tucked in. Only when they went downstairs a few minutes later did she realize how everything had affected him, as well. He looked completely drained as they entered the courtyard, his face a reflection of the sadness he was clearly feeling, his eyes too bleak for her to endure. She didn't understand his reaction, but she knew it was genuine. She'd seen the same black look in her own eyes.

The smell of homemade bread filled the terrace as they walked outside, the cries of the children echoing off the sun-streaked walls.

"Let's go in here," she said, pointing to one of the buildings. "It'll be cooler and quieter than the cafeteria."

He followed her into a room filled with sewing machines. She answered his unspoken question.

"They make most of their clothes," she said, "but they also do embroidery to sell and make money." She picked up a square of cotton, edged in lace. "These are pillowcases. They decorate them and peddle them downtown for a quarter apiece."

Ignoring her explanation, he took the bed linen from her hands and put it down on a table nearby. "Why do you do this?" he asked. "Why do you torture yourself like this?"

"I love the children," she answered. "They need my help. Why not?"

"But surely it hurts?"

"It would hurt more to never be around them." She looked at him curiously. "And don't say you don't understand. I know you do. I can see it in your eyes."

She watched him struggle with an answer. After a long moment, he spoke. "I'm not the man I used to be, Emma. At one time, yes, I wanted to have a family, a home, a wife." His voice turned husky. "But that didn't work out...and it's not something I've thought about in a very long time."

"What happened?" she asked quietly.

He lifted his gaze to hers, and it was so full of anger, she took a step back. He blinked and the emotion disappeared. Had she imagined it? "It's not worth talking about," he said tightly.

Even though she knew it wasn't a good idea, Emma started to press him. At that moment, though, two of the children rushed in, each holding a huge bowl of soup with slabs of bread perched on the side of the plate. They ate in silence, and when they were finished, Raul stood. "Shall we go into town?"

THEY WALKED up and down the narrow cobbled streets of Samaipata, peering into dark shops and stopping on the corners to admire the work of local artisans, who were sitting on blankets on the hard sidewalks amid their wares. The festival and parade gave everyone a chance to show off their talents, and they were selling everything from handmade flutes and carved gourds to delicate gold jewelry. Raul insisted on buying it all, and by the time the sun had slipped behind the mountains, they were loaded once more with gifts to take back to the orphanage.

Throughout the afternoon, Emma tried to reconcile Reina's gossip with the generous, kind man beside her, but failed. When he finally suggested they stop for a drink before the parade began, Emma knew the time had arrived. She had to know the truth.

They picked a café on the square, facing the

cathedral. A dozen or so tables lined the windows, each set with mismatched chairs, no two alike. Dark beams supported the low ceiling, and a long, wooden bar took up one side of the room. Two cats, sitting inside one of the windows licking each other, briefly stopped to inspect the new arrivals, then returned to their more important task of grooming.

Emma and Raul took the table nearest the front door, and a waiter appeared immediately. Raul gave him their drink order, then excused himself to go to the rest room. Emma felt as if she'd been granted a reprieve. She didn't *want* to ask him about his past. She wanted to accept him just as he was. The warmth in his eyes, the taste of his lips, the way he knew what she was feeling simply by looking at her—those were the only things that counted. Weren't they?

Just as the waiter placed her cola in front of her and Raul's drink on the other side of the table, she sensed someone walking up behind her. Expecting Raul, she turned, and her eyes widened in shock.

William Kelman smiled back.

''Ms. Toussaint! I don't believe it. What a co-incidence!''

Was it? The question popped into her mind without a warning, and she immediately chastised herself. What else could it be but coincidence? He might be strange, but William Kelman wasn't psychic, she was sure. And there was no way he could have followed them—all the way from Santa Cruz—and she not notice.

"Mr. Kelman. What a surprise to see you here. Are you in town for the festival?"

He nodded. "Yes, I drove down this morning. Dreadful road, isn't it?" He started to pull out Raul's chair and sit down, then he saw the drink and stopped. "You're with a friend—I won't intrude."

She opened her mouth to reply, but before she could speak, he squatted beside the table.

"I won't intrude," he said, "but I will take advantage of the moment."

She replied in the only way she could, her stomach turning over in a wave of anxiety. "What can I do for you?"

His eyes seemed to grow a little bluer, a little colder. "I was wondering if you've had a chance to rethink the opportunity we discussed last week. It's still a viable option, you know."

"I *have* been thinking about it," she said, stalling for time.

"Good, good." His expression held no warmth, although he was smiling.

A vision formed in her mind of her children moving farther and farther away from her. "My answer hasn't changed."

He let the words lie between them for a moment. "You're making a mistake," he said finally.

"I'm sorry you feel that way. But I'm sure you understand my position."

"I understand. But I'm not sure *you* do." He stared at her for a while, then stood. "I'm very disappointed we couldn't come to an agreement. I think we could have helped each other."

"I'd still be happy to help you." She gripped her drink so hard she was surprised the glass didn't shatter. She was giving up the best opportunity she'd ever had to get her children back, but she couldn't do it this way. "I have to work within the confines of the system, though."

He shook his head almost regretfully. "I thought you had goals, things you needed to accomplish. I guess I was wrong."

She froze. "I'm sorry?"

His eyes pierced hers. "Don't you need money, Ms. Toussaint?"

"Everyone needs money," she said.

"But you have a special reason for it, don't you?"

She rose quickly, so quickly the table shook as she bumped it on her way up.

He held out his hands and stopped her from speaking. "I needed some help and I thought you needed money. A trade seemed like the way to accomplish both goals. No need to get excited. I thought this was the way to do it, but obviously it isn't.''

"You're right. And my private life is just that— private. I'd appreciate it if you'd recognize that fact.''

"Of course.'' He stepped away from the table, both hands in front of him, just as Raul approached from behind.

Emma held her breath as Kelman turned and the two men stared at each other.

Raul spoke first. He wasn't surprised to see Kelman, she realized, or if he was, he kept it from his demeanor. His tone was casual, his voice low. "Hello, Kelman.''

Something—surprise? dismay?—flared in Kelman's eyes as he looked from Emma to Raul, then back to her. He'd known she was with someone else—he'd noted the glass—but he definitely had not expected that other person to be Raul. As improbable as it had to be, Emma had the fleeting thought that he'd planned the encounter, arranged it so he could approach her when she wasn't expecting him. But how could he have known she was coming here? It didn't make sense. Before she could think about it further, Kelman ducked his head in Raul's direction. "Santos,'' he said.

The silence that built was full of tension. From where she stood, Emma could see it in every line of Raul's body and in the mask that Kelman wore.

The older man finally spoke. "I won't keep you," he said, his gaze directed at Emma once more. "But I will be talking to you. Perhaps we can work something out."

She nodded stiffly, at a loss for what to say.

Raul spoke as soon as the other man left the table. "Where did he come from? I didn't see him earlier."

"I don't know. I was sitting here and he just appeared. Said he'd come for the festival."

"What did he want?" Raul asked the question with no special intonation. She heard the strain, though.

"It's a business thing," she answered. Her voice was equally blasé, but beneath the table, her knees still trembled. She couldn't tell if it was fear or anger—or the realization that her goals were more out of reach than ever. "I really can't go into it."

He didn't answer, and in the quiet, she remembered his words. *You can trust me.* Without any warning at all, she suddenly wanted to pour out her heart and tell him what had happened. To ask his advice. Kelman's words had left her breathless, but now she was confused. Was she imagining things or had the man really been talking about her children? It seemed impossible for him to know her background—Reina knew, yet would have never told him—but what else could he have been referring to? And even more importantly, why?

She started to speak, then all at once, the parade began with firecrackers and booming music. A colorful crowd of marchers—and watchers—surged into the street just outside the windows. Conversation was now impossible. The café, so silent a second before, filled almost instantly with the overflow from outside, the narrow walkways suddenly packed as the procession reached the closest corner.

Emma turned to watch, her words on hold. On the shoulders of half-a-dozen men, now coming up the pavement, rested a statue of the orphanage's patron saint. Painted in bright colors and tinted with gold leaf, the carved wooden image commanded a position above the throng. Behind it, the girls walked hand in hand, their white dresses starched and ironed, gleaming in the dying light of evening.

Above the music and shouts of the crowd was another noise, something more pressing. Emma looked at the clouds over the cathedral. Just as she did, a jagged streak of lightning lit up the sky. A moment later, the rain began.

THEY REMAINED in the café while the crowds in front of the window fled from the downpour. Raul studied Emma as they waited. She could feel his steady stare and knew he wanted to ask her what was going on with Kelman. But he didn't.

After an hour, it was clear the rain was not going to quit. It came down in sheets, cold and without mercy. The street was already flooded, the muddy water floating over the curb to splash along the sidewalk. They discussed the situation, Raul deciding finally they couldn't wait any longer. He dashed outside into the rain to retrieve the truck only to return a short time later with bad news.

"There's something wrong with the Rover." He shook his head, which sent out a flurry of raindrops. "I can't get it started. I seriously doubt I can get it looked at this late, either. Is there somewhere we could stay the night?"

Her pulse quickened. "There's a small hotel over by the orphanage."

"I suggest we head for it," he said, his dark eyes gleaming. "There doesn't seem to be another alternative right now."

She nodded once, her eyes on his. If there *was* a different option, she didn't really want to know what it was.

The small hotel had been a convent a hundred years before. They ran into the lobby, dripping wet from their dash from the cab they'd taken. With cash in hand, Raul quickly made his way to the front of the line, and a minute later, he returned with two keys.

They followed the bellboy out of the lobby and down a dark corridor. After a few minutes of twist-

ing turns and blind corners, the hallway unexpectedly opened into an interior atrium. The wind and
rain hadn't relented and, in fact, seemed to be
growing. The roses planted in the tiny, protected
area whipped about under the cruel onslaught, their
bloodred blossoms trembling as they brushed the
ground. The temperature had dropped, as well, and
Emma found herself shivering.

They continued down the hallway, making so
many more turns that Emma was completely dis-
oriented. She thought she saw movement out of the
corner of her eye, but it was only shadows, perhaps
the ghosts of the long-ago nuns. Finally, at the end
of one particularly dark corridor, the bellboy
stopped in front of a set of double doors. They
looked heavy and solid, and were made of carved
wood. Taking Emma's key, he unlocked them and
pushed them open to reveal a tiny room.

It was as spare as it had been when the nuns
lived in it. Whitewashed walls. One lone window
set high up. Two twin beds with a small chest between them. A single door led to an even smaller
bathroom. There was nothing else.

"It's all they had," Raul told her. "Mine's
down the hall—even smaller, they said."

"This is fine," she said. "Just fine."

But it wasn't.

It was lonely and stark and totally without
warmth. She'd go nuts in there by herself, and she

didn't like it a bit. She wanted one room and one big bed.

And Raul's arms around her the whole night long.

He looked down at her, and that was all it took. He turned and gave the bellboy a handful of *bolivianos* and the key to the other room. Neither of them heard the doors close.

CHAPTER TWELVE

EMMA DIDN'T SPEAK. She simply moved into his arms and laid her head against his chest. Raul wanted to tell her to stop, that what they were doing was wrong, that she'd hate him later, but he couldn't. She was too beautiful and too warm and too sexy, and if keeping secrets from her was what he had to do, then he'd just have to add that to his growing list of sins and pray for mercy later.

He folded his arms around her and pulled her closer. Kelman had done or said something while Raul had been away from the table, and it had sent Emma over the edge. He was a bastard for knowing this and taking advantage of it, but he was a man, as well. He'd been able to think of little else but holding her in his arms ever since the last time they'd made love.

She moved into his embrace and made a sound deep in her throat, a sound that echoed inside him, then she lifted her face to his and started to speak. He stopped her by kissing her. Whatever she wanted to tell him, he didn't want to know. All he wanted was to feel her body against his and some-

how ease the pain he saw in her eyes. Nothing else
mattered but that. The feel of her lips, so soft and
giving, swept away the very last chance he had at
resisting.

She accepted his kiss and opened her mouth to
his. Beneath her sweet taste, he could sense her
trembling desire. She wanted to forget as much as
he wanted to erase.

They stood that way for another moment, consumed with the need to feel, then Raul picked her
up and carried her across the tiny room to one of
the beds. He set her down and began to undo her
buttons, but she shook her head almost impatiently
and replaced his fingers with her own. In seconds,
she'd shed her blouse and her slacks and stood
before him in a pale pink bra and panties edged
with lace.

She was so beautiful, so perfect, and all she
wanted from him was himself. She wasn't getting
who she thought she was, though. Once he had
been a man a woman like her might have loved,
but not now. He was too hard, too cold, too un-
forgiving. Women like Emma Toussaint didn't
make love with the kind of man he'd become, but
he wasn't about to tell her that.

Instead, in the cold darkness of the tiny hotel
room, as the thunder rumbled and the rain
pounded, he took off his own clothes. And then he
reached for her.

HIS HANDS WERE COLD as they gripped her shoulders, but almost immediately, they warmed against the heat of her skin. Emma let Raul bring her closer, the wall of his chest flattening her breasts. The first time they'd made love she'd registered nothing but the passion inside her. This time, the details came into focus. His body was lean, hard and trim. Underneath the expensive clothing and polished appearance, he had the physique of a man accustomed to physical labor. She wondered about it briefly, then all thoughts fled as she was consumed by the sensations assaulting her—his fingers brushing her neck, his mouth pressing her own, his broad back beneath her hands.

Once again, his touch was magic, and the feel of his heated caress was more than she could handle. He seemed to sense her reaction and started to pull back...but she tightened her hands on his waist and murmured her assent. He moaned his own answer and cradled the back of her head in his hand, kissing her even more deeply, demanding she give just as much.

And so she gave—her tongue sought his, and her fingertips smoothed his body. She couldn't get enough of him, couldn't fill herself with his strength as quickly as her heart demanded. Her hands flitted over his body, stopping here and there, the contact both hot and cold at once. He met each of her strokes with one of his own, his hands playing against her skin and making her tremble with a need she hadn't ever known until meeting Raul.

A moment later, he lowered her to the bed behind them. The rest of her clothing—the bra and panties—disappeared under his expert touch until there was nothing between them. In the barest light coming through the high window overhead, his dark muscles gleamed against her pale skin.

After that, it was all a blur. She felt him kissing her, felt him touching her most private parts, felt herself giving to him everything she'd been holding back. Her secrets, her pain, every hurt and every ache, she relinquished them all to the heat of Raul's passion. He took them, as she'd known he would, and turned them into pure desire.

His mouth covering hers, he rolled over on the bed and brought her to her side, tucking her back against his front. It was the only way they could both fit on the bed, but it didn't matter to Emma. She was past the point of caring. All she could think about was the heat of his body as it pressed into hers. From her shoulders to her hips, to the bottoms of her feet, she felt consumed by this man—which was exactly what she wanted.

He threw a leg over her hip and she responded, fitting her body more comfortably against his. He rained kisses on her bare back, sending shivers up and down her spine. Reaching around, he cupped one breast and then the other. His touch was urgent and grew even more so as it slipped downward.

As his fingers came to the juncture of her thighs, she arched into his hand with a gasp. He murmured in her ear, his breath at once hot and sweet as he spoke. Her name, she realized through a haze. He was saying her name. Then she heard nothing, nothing but the blood rushing in her veins, nothing but her pulse as it roared, nothing but the call of her heart as he moved his hand quickly and increased the rhythm of his touch. She cried out and collapsed against him.

He didn't wait for her to recover. Instead, he coaxed her around to face him. Limp with desire, she stared into his eyes. They were black and endless, and in them she read what she'd suspected all along. He was as lost as she was, and needed this almost more. Reaching down between them she grasped his erection with her hand. He was already prepared. She guided him toward her and a moment later her world exploded.

EMMA WOKE UP in the middle of the night, gasping and desperate. The room was so dark she felt as if she were underwater, in a tunnel, with no way out. Her heart pounding with fear, she struggled up from the twisted covers and started to scream.

Then Raul reached for her. "Emma…Emma. It's okay, darling. Calm down!"

The words reached through the panic and returned her to reality. She fell back against the mattress, her pulse still racing, her breath coming fast. "Oh, God..." she moaned. "I...I didn't know where I was for a minute. It was so dark..."

He patted her bare shoulder comfortingly, then pulled her closer to him. The bed seemed even smaller now than it had been when they were making love, but she didn't mind. She wanted to absorb as much of his warmth and presence as she could.

"It's okay," he said again. "It's all right."

She laughed, a little self-conscious. "I'm sorry. I woke up and I didn't know where I was. I didn't mean to wake you."

"You didn't," he answered. "I was already awake."

She turned his wrist to look at his watch. "It's 2 a.m. Why weren't you sleeping?"

He took a slow, deep breath. She could feel his chest rise with the movement, and behind the motion she felt the weight of a decision he seemed to be making. She tensed.

"I was thinking..." he said.

"About what?"

"About you," he answered. "And William Kelman."

She lay perfectly still within his arms.

"I want to know what's going on between the two of you. It's time for you to tell me."

"I could say the same," she shot back. "I think you share some secrets with him, as well."

He propped himself up with his elbow, then reached out with his other hand and pulled her chin toward him. When she was finally facing him, he spoke again. "William Kelman and I go back a very long way. I know what kind of man he is. Do I need to say more?"

"I don't know," Emma replied. Her heart was doing a funny dance. "Is there more?"

"Yes…but it's not important."

"I don't believe you. I think it's very important."

He ignored her. "Tell me what's going on between you two."

She shook her head, then stopped. She'd just shared her body with this man, her body and her passion. Like some kind of a surgeon, he'd taken the pain from her heart, excised it cleanly—if only for a little while. She owed him.

But not this.

"I can't," she said quietly. "What happens in my office has to stay there. It's the same kind of trust you talked to me about before—that's what I have to have between myself and my clients."

"Even if I can help you?"

"You can't," she said bluntly. "No one can."

His eyes pierced hers in the darkness. "I know

men like Kelman,'' he told her. ''I've fought them, too.''

''It doesn't matter, anyway.'' She shook her head. ''It's over.''

''Did he win?''

''Win?'' She looked at him curiously. ''No...I wouldn't say he won. But it wasn't some kind of contest or anything.''

''Maybe not to you.'' His expression was grim.

A shiver passed through her. ''What do you mean?''

''He's not the type to give up, Emma. If you didn't provide him with what he wanted, whatever it was, he'll return—and stay until he gets it.''

''I don't think so.''

He had his hand on her arm, and when she answered, his grip tightened almost painfully. ''Listen to me,'' he said. ''You don't know this man like I do. He's ruthless. You need to tell me what's going on. I can help you.''

Something in his voice scared her. It was his intensity, she realized with a start. It was as strong as the passion they'd shared a few hours earlier. She pulled away and stared at him, then almost immediately, he seemed to realize what he was doing. He backed down, but only slightly.

''He uses people, Emma, and he doesn't care who gets hurt as long as he gets what he wants.

I've known lots of men like him, but he's the worst.''

Emma took a deep breath. "Did you know these men…in prison?''

In the tiny line of light coming through the nearby window, his eyes glittered. "Why do you ask me that?''

"I've heard things," she answered. "Santa Cruz is a small town. There's gossip.''

"Would you care if it was true?''

She'd already asked herself that question, but the answer was as elusive as ever. "I don't know,'' she confessed.

"Then take it for what it is, and someday, if you still care, I'll explain. Right now, you need to think about what's going on, and it boils down to this—if William Kelman is doing something he shouldn't be, and you're involved, you need to tell me.''

He waited for her to say something—anything—but no words came. She was relieved he hadn't answered her question, relieved yet frightened, and she struggled to know how to respond. Finally, he reached out and pulled her closer. With his hands on her body and her name on his breath, he took her back to the place where she felt safest….

THE DAWN WAS so beautiful it seemed as if the night before had been a dream. Raul would have thought he'd fantasized it all, except for the evidence—Emma sleeping beside him when he'd awoken.

He'd been tempted to tell her the truth earlier, the words right on his tongue. Who Kelman really was. How he'd framed him. What he would do to her, allowed half a chance.

But the fragile trust she'd given him would be instantly destroyed by that harsh reality. Emma was a smart woman, and she would figure out everything immediately. The consequence of that was obvious; she would never forgive him, and both of them would lose. He'd never get Kelman. And that was still his main goal, right?

No, Raul was going to have to hope for the best—that he'd be able to protect her when the time came and Kelman's trap was sprung.

And there *was* a trap. There had to be, even if she wouldn't tell Raul it was. He eased himself up in the bed and slowly pulled away from Emma's still form. Reaching for her purse, he dug around until he found the proof he needed. The small black disk, disguised as a button, gleamed malevolently in the darkness.

A bug.

Kelman had had his man bump into Emma in the street to distract her. Then he'd slipped the tracking device into her purse and she hadn't even known it. It was the only way he could have found her in Samaipata. But he hadn't counted on Raul.

He looked at the tiny disk in the palm of his hand and nodded his head. This explained the truck. He hadn't wanted to upset Emma, so he'd kept it to himself, but someone had tampered with the engine; it hadn't been a simple mechanical breakdown that had stranded them last night. Now he understood. But why keep them here in Samaipata? The question left Raul uneasy.

Levering his thumbnail under the rim of the bug, he popped the plastic edges apart. The wires were thin and he snapped them with one twist.

Emma stirred as he put the bug back together and dropped it into her purse. When she finally opened her eyes, he was sitting in the chair opposite the bed, looking at her.

"You're awake already," she said. "Don't you ever sleep?"

He shook his head. "Not when there's a beautiful woman nearby."

In the subtle light of early morning, she smiled softly, sensually. "If that's how you feel, then what are you doing on the other side of the room?"

He answered her by putting the rest of his thoughts on hold, and crossing the space between them.

THE COBBLESTONE STREETS were washed and clean. Raul had left the hotel early and found a mechanic, and now Emma, heading for the newly repaired Range Rover, bag in hand, listened as the peal of the cathedral bells filled the square. The air felt different than it had yesterday, sharper and fresher, but glancing at Raul, Emma realized she was mistaken; it wasn't the air that was different. It was her.

For the first time in a very long time, she felt a ray of hope. It was silly, really. Not a single thing had actually changed, but somehow she thought it might. Kelman's offer was behind her, and despite Raul's warning, she believed that problem was solved. She would just work harder...then work some more. The money she needed would come somehow.

They visited the orphanage to deliver the presents they'd bought the afternoon before, and soon they were on the road back to Santa Cruz. The pavement, crumbling and old, was washed out in places, but generally passable, and the hours flew by.

After a while, Raul glanced at Emma from across the truck. "Will you ever go back to New Orleans and live?"

The passing jungle was a blur of green as she turned to meet his eyes. "Absolutely," she answered. "My mom's gone, but it's home. I miss it a lot."

"And after that?"

"I don't know. I haven't really given it any

thought. Everything I think about stops at the point I get my kids back.''

''What if you lose the appeal?''

''Losing is not an option.''

He shook his head. ''Losing is always an option, Emma. You need to think about that, you know.''

She refused even to consider the possibility. ''Did you handle these kinds of cases when you were an attorney?''

''I did it all.'' His hands gripped the steering wheel as he slowed to go around a huge hole in the road.

When he said nothing else, she realized belatedly that this was how he must have felt when she'd avoided all his questions. She forced away the queries flooding her mind. He was someone to be with for the moment, she told herself. Someone she could share her pain with, but not her life.

Someone she could be with...but not love.

He interrupted her thoughts with a question about Bolivia. She shook her head in exasperation.

''It's a very poor country,'' she said. ''They'll never become a more powerful force until they get rid of their corruption.''

''Is it bad?''

''The worst,'' she answered. ''Everything is tainted, every government office, every business transaction, everything. What do you think of the country so far?''

"I've lived a lot of places," he answered, his voice noncommittal. "But I think I'll stay here for a while. It's not that bad a place, and there's no good reason for me to go back to the States."

His answer struck her hard, primarily because it reinforced her earlier thoughts. There could never be anything permanent between the two of them— even if she wanted it; she wouldn't be overseas and away from home for a moment longer than she had to, and he was one of those men she often saw at the bank. Men with money who were simply passing through. She thought of them as permanent expatriates. They had no anchors and there was nothing to hold them down—no families, no friends, no necessary jobs—and so they wandered, looking for something but not knowing what. It made her sad to think of Raul in those terms, because he wasn't truly that type of man. Remembering his earlier actions at the orphanage, she knew he should have a wife and children; fatherhood would suit him well.

It was late by the time they pulled up in front of Emma's home, darkness edging into the yard and the house itself. Raul parked the truck, then walked to Emma's side of the vehicle. Opening her door, he helped her out. As soon as they stepped into the entryway, she turned and began to say goodbye.

He shook his head. "You're not getting rid of

me that easily,'' he said, his voice low and liquid. ''I can't leave just like that.''

She looked up at him, desire twisting deep inside her. Let him in or keep him out? The question seemed a simple one, but there were too many layers surrounding it to count.

He read her hesitation. ''If you don't want me to stay, I won't. I'll leave right now.''

''I don't know what I want,'' she confessed. ''You probably find that hard to believe after last night, but it's the truth.''

He lifted his hands and cradled her face, his thumb drawing a line around her mouth. Then he lowered his head to hers, his mouth suddenly pressing against her own, his tongue insistent. The kiss was like all his others—hot and demanding— and she was breathless when he finally pulled back. Todd had never left her reeling like this, nor had any other man, she thought with dazed amazement. But she could get used to it.

''It's your choice.'' His voice was hoarse and the sound of it rasped over her, leaving her trembling, just like his touch. ''I'll leave. You decide.''

Her heart screamed *leave,* but her body cried *stay.*

She hesitated a moment longer, then she lifted her arms and wrapped them around his neck. He closed the door behind him with a kick.

SHORTLY AFTER ONE in the morning, Emma walked Raul downstairs and let him out the front door. The street was silent and dark, a few clouds scudding across the moon, the hibiscus blooms rippling in the breeze. The only sound was her neighbor's birds. In addition to his monkey, the man had an aviary in his garden filled with wild macaws and yellow-and-green parrots. The creatures' cries, sharp and savage, lent a sense of unreality to the moment. Raul paused at the gate and kissed her, his lips so addictive she found it hard to let him go. He seemed to feel the same way, and only after a while could he finally tear himself away.

"I have to take care of some business in the morning," he said, his hand on her neck. "Can I call you at the office?"

"I'd like that," she answered. "I'll be there."

He nodded, kissed her again, then climbed into the truck. She watched him drive down the street. She hadn't really wanted him to leave, but she needed to be alone after all their time together. She had to sort out her feelings, and she couldn't do that with him in her bed.

Trudging back up the stairs a few minutes later, Emma went into her bathroom and began to draw water for a bath. The steam from the tub had just reached the mirror when she heard a noise downstairs. She twisted the taps off at once, and the sound repeated itself. It was louder this time, and more insistent. Finally she understood; someone was knocking on the front door. Pounding on it, in fact, as if he wanted to break it down.

She grabbed her robe from the hook on the door and wrapped it around her, her racing heart mimicking the noise downstairs. Had Raul forgotten something? If he had, how had he gotten past the gate? And she doubted he would make the kind of racket that was coming up from the foyer now, but she bounded down the stairs just the same, her bare feet slapping across the wooden floor as she ran. The knocking didn't cease until she threw open the door.

Six policemen stood on her front porch. Dressed in green fatigues, they each carried an automatic gun and wore belligerent frowns. Behind them, the iron gate swung crazily, the top hinge completely broken off.

Emma's mouth dropped open. "What in the world—"

Interrupting her, the man in front spoke her name, his gaze insolent as it took in her robe. He wore extra gold braid across his shoulders and a cap with an insignia on it. He was blue-chinned and rough-looking. Threatening.

"Señorita Toussaint? Emma Toussaint?"

"Y-yes?" With a shaking hand, she pulled together the thick lapels of her housecoat. "What is it?" she asked. "What's wrong?"

He pushed the door back with one hand and stepped inside, forcing her backward. ''We're here to search your home,'' he announced. ''We've been told you have drugs.''

CHAPTER THIRTEEN

EMMA STARED at him in shock, unable to speak. When she finally found her voice, she wished she hadn't. But it was too late; she couldn't take back her astonished reply.

"Drugs? Here? Are you insane?"

His reaction wasn't the one she expected. He smiled. "*No, señorita, no estoy loco.* But you may be by the time we finish."

The men behind him snickered at his wit, but Emma went silent with astonishment. He stalked arrogantly past her, then lifted his hand and waved it toward her living room, tilting his head to the man directly behind him. "You go in there." Pointing in other directions, he told the rest of them to scatter, as well.

"Stop!" Terrified and shaking, Emma made her voice a strident screech. She had to act angry; to show her fear to these men could be a fatal flaw. "You can't do this! You can't come in here and start searching like this."

Unbelievably, no one paid her any attention. She could have been speaking Farsi for all the notice her words garnered. As if she didn't exist, the policeman did as he was instructed and stomped over Emma's silk rug to disappear into the darkness of the front room. Immediately something shattered.

Emma whirled and glowered at the man who'd stayed behind, the one in charge. "What do you think you're doing? This is crazy! Who told you there were drugs here?"

"Our informants are confidential. You don't need to know." He lifted his weapon toward the second floor. "What's up there?"

From the back of the house, the kitchen it seemed, came another crash. Ignoring the man beside her, Emma took two steps in that direction, then felt herself yanked back. She looked down, her jaw dropping open again, at the policeman's hand on her arm.

"I asked you a question," he said, roughly shaking her. "What's upstairs?"

For a second she was stunned, then she recovered...and recoiled, jerking her arm. He held on tightly, his fingers digging sharply into her flesh. "Tell me!"

"It's my bedroom." Her heart racing, she spoke furiously. "Now turn me loose or—"

Without another word, he spun her around and shoved her toward the stairs. "Let's go," he said. "Right now."

From over her shoulder, Emma stared at him in

a daze. His eyes were narrow and small, and his expression held only grim determination. "Go!"

Emma took the stairs as slowly as possible, buying herself time. She had to think! She had to have a plan! Nothing came except panic, and by the time they reached the second floor, she could hardly breathe her chest was so tight.

Another clatter from downstairs sounded as they entered her bedroom. Emma flinched at the noise, the smell of her perfume sickeningly sweet as it wafted into the bedroom from the bath she'd been filling when the police arrived. She turned to the man behind her, her stomach cramping in fear. "Look all you want. You're not going to find a thing."

He hesitated just a second—long enough to make her mouth go even drier—then he walked to her dresser and pulled out the first drawer. Dumping the contents—her T-shirts and shorts—onto the floor, he kicked them around with one booted foot, then went to the next drawer. In a matter of minutes, all of her clothing lay in a jumble on the carpet beneath his feet.

He bent down and ran his hand along the interior of the now-exposed piece of furniture. There was nothing there, and he straightened a moment later. In short order, he ripped through the rest of her bedroom, pulling the sheets from the mattress, turning it upside down, going through everything in her desk.

She stood by helplessly and watched, her heart threatening to leap from between her ribs, her hands clamped at her sides. Starting toward her bathroom, he stopped abruptly when a shout from downstairs could be heard.

"¡Jefe—baje! ¡Immediatamente!" Chief—come downstairs! Right now!

He sent her a look of pure satisfaction, using his gun to gesture toward the stair, and smirked. "Let's go, *señorita*. To see what my men have not found."

"There's nothing down there."

"Then you have nothing to fear. *Pase, por favor.*"

With a faint buzz in her ears, Emma headed for the stairs. The policeman was right behind her; she could smell him, onions and beer and unwashed clothing. Her agitation mingled with his odor, and her stomach threatened to erupt. At the very last minute, she managed to fight the nausea.

The dissonance of the men's voices led them to Emma's kitchen. As she stepped through the doorway, she gasped, her gaze taking in the havoc they'd created in their search. One man, standing in the middle of it all, caught her attention. His voice was gleeful.

"¡Mire, Jefe! See what I found!"

Shock stole Emma's breath. She told herself to breathe, told herself to stay calm. But any chance she had at composure was hijacked by cold, stark horror as, with a triumphant grin, the policeman held up a plastic bag.

It was full of something white and powdery.

THERE WERE NO LIGHTS ON inside the house; it probably didn't have electricity, Raul surmised. Sitting outside the hovel belonging to the man who'd planted the bug in Emma's bag, Raul took a chance and lit his small cigar, cupping his hand around the flame to hide it from sight. He had planned on stopping by the barrio one way or the other, but this had worked out just fine. It made no sense to go home; he had too much on his mind to sleep.

With Emma's scent still on his hands and her voice lingering in his mind, he couldn't focus, couldn't concentrate. The smoke from the cigar drifted up in a wisp before his face, as he thought about what that signified.

It'd been a long time since a woman had meant anything to him, such a long time he wasn't sure that was what he was experiencing. The weekend had been a revelation to him, though. Emma Toussaint was a special person, and she had all the qualities he would have looked for in a woman in his other life. Intelligence. Honesty. Passion. He could actually love her, he realized with a start, if that was what he was looking for.

The first time they'd made love it'd been purely physical. This time something else had happened, something he hadn't wanted. He'd felt himself drawn to Emma in an emotional way. He cared what happened to her, cared if she got her children back, cared if she got tangled up in Kelman's web.

His eyes on the house before him, Raul pulled deeply on the cigar, the smoke filling his lungs with a sharp bite. He'd give it another five minutes, then he'd go inside.

Maybe by then, he'd have Emma out of his mind and back in the place where she belonged. He wasn't sure where that was—but it could not be his heart.

THE HANDCUFFS cut into her wrists with a cold metallic bite. Emma squirmed against their clasp and told herself it didn't matter, but she failed. Their pinch *did* hurt, and she was terrified. Sitting in the back of a Bolivian police car was the last place she had ever imagined being, and the drug search they'd conducted to get her there was too stunning even to consider. The enormity of it all had barely begun to sink in, and she knew why: denial was her only hope, at this point. Otherwise, she'd collapse.

There was only one problem. Her refusal to accept the situation wasn't working.

The car swerved to miss a speeding taxi, then they took the next corner on two wheels, heading off the nearest ring and straight for downtown. She'd never seen the police station in Santa Cruz and had no idea what to expect. On the other hand, she'd never been arrested in the United States, either. All bets were off, that much she knew. A phone call, a plea for help, any chance she'd get some assistance depended purely on the whims of the men in the front seat. Bolivia was a republic, but that didn't mean democracy ruled.

Before they'd left her house, she'd tried to call Raul. Sneaking the portable phone into the closet with her, she'd dialed his number as she'd grabbed a pair of jeans and shirt. The effort had produced only near heart failure when the officer in charge had come in unexpectedly. Yelling at her to hurry up, he'd failed to notice the phone she'd thrown into a pile of clothing already on the floor. She had no idea where Raul might have gone after he'd left her house, but he hadn't been home.

Now they were slowing down and she still had no plan.

The car stopped in front of what she assumed was the *cuartelillo de policia*. It looked like the rest of the official buildings she'd seen in town; a grim two-story stuccoed block with a severe brick front and a few dirty windows facing the street. The two officers in the front seat climbed out of the vehicle, their coarse laughter echoing in the humid night air. They moved slowly; only when they got behind the wheel were South Americans in a hurry. Finally one of the men opened the rear door of the police car, grabbed her arm and pulled her roughly from the back seat. Emma's shoulder screamed in protest, but fear—absolute, blood-thinning, heart-stopping fear—kept her from speaking.

They dragged her up the sidewalk and into the building, passing through a lobby even bleaker than the exterior, an empty, echoing chamber with nothing but a desk and a single chair behind it. She heard the distant sound of phones ringing and laughter, but no one else was in sight as the two men herded her toward the rear of the building. Reaching the last door, they pushed it open.

Blinking, she saw what appeared to be a sort of reception area, dirty and crowded with other men in uniforms. They were all talking, their voices as loud and rough as the two men beside her. A numbing disbelief swelled inside her as she swung her head from one side to the other and looked at the room and the men who filled it. Terror, unlike anything she'd ever felt before, rose inside her, as well. One or two of them turned and briefly stared at her, then they went back to what they were doing, her presence so insignificant it didn't even warrant a second glance.

Later, she realized she should have known at that point. But she was too numb and too frightened to understand. Only afterward did she figure it out.

By then, it was too late.

RAUL EASED THE TRUCK door open and climbed out, shutting it behind him with a soft click. The moon had disappeared completely. Crossing the yard in front of the hut, he thanked God for the darkness and the poverty. The people who lived here didn't look outside when their dogs barked. They didn't dare.

He made his way toward the tiny house, then slipped through the inky darkness to the backyard, the smell of charred beef—someone's dinner— hanging in the air. He moved slowly, stealthily, until he reached the rear door. It was propped open with a pile of handmade bricks, the night air welcomed for its breeze, its humidity ignored.

Pausing by the entry, he allowed his eyes to adjust as he stared inside. The house had a single room, one corner the kitchen, the other a bedroom, a small cot tucked against the wall. The man had no family. Raul had watched him for several days after he'd followed Emma, and no one else had come in or gone out of the hut. The man slept soundly on the bed, his raucous snores competing with the howls of a neighborhood dog. Raul could have driven his truck straight into the room, and the guy would never have heard him. An empty liter bottle of beer rested at a crazy angle by his feet.

Raul shook his head in disgust, then he walked into the hovel and knocked over the stack of bricks, slamming the door shut behind him.

As the sound reached his ears, the man struggled up from his stupor, his confusion evident. *"¿Qué—?"*

He had no time to say anything else. Raul's kick landed exactly where he'd planned—on the man's hand as he reached under his mattress. He screamed a curse, his voice filled with pain, and jerked back his hand.

Raul reached under the stained and dirty bed and pulled out the .38 the drunk had been trying to get. The fetid smell of beer wafted up between them as Raul pressed the muzzle of the pistol into the man's cheek. Above the dull black metal, his eyes rounded.

"I want to know about your friend, *amigo*. The one who hired you to follow the blonde." Raul's voice was calm and cool, his Spanish perfect. "Talk to me, *por favor*."

THE NARROW WALKWAY smelled even worse than the two men pressing in behind Emma. It was dark, too. A single, bare bulb, hanging from two wires, offered the only illumination. She stumbled slightly, then straightened and yanked herself away from the policeman who reached toward her. A second later, they stopped her in front of a scratched and dirty door. It had a window too high to see into and more locks on the outside than she had time to count. Within seconds, one of the men had them all undone, and they opened the door and pushed her inside.

Before Emma could get her bearings, she stumbled again and immediately hit her shin on something sharp, losing her balance completely in the dimness. Crying out, she fell to the floor, turning at the very last second to land on her shoulder, instead of her face. The maneuver didn't help; the concrete was hard and cold when it rose up to meet her with a sickening jolt.

Stunned, Emma lay motionless until the smell beneath her registered. She gagged and quickly rolled over, scrambling to her feet, her wrists still handcuffed behind her.

The room was minuscule—not even as big as her closet—and filthy, an open drain in the center of it, the source of the gut-wrenching odor. A scarred, wooden table and two broken-down metal chairs listed near the doorway. One of the chairs lay on its side—she'd obviously run into it—a leg now dangling by a single screw. The only light came from the square of glass set in the door at her back, yet it was enough to see the walls. They were scratched and nasty, the paint too old to tell the color beneath the jumble of desperate messages the room's former occupants had managed to scrawl.

With a hopeless moan, she closed her eyes and began to sob.

IT DIDN'T TAKE too long.

Within a matter of minutes, Raul had the man talking, but he certainly didn't like what he had to say.

"Señor Kelman hired me, *sí, sí.* I went into her house once just to check it out, and I...I put the bug in the lady's purse, but that's it. Nothing else." His eyes were too wide and frightened for him to be telling anything but the truth, and Raul let his fingers open slightly. The man's breathing was rapid and shallow as he clawed at his collar, still tight against his neck.

"What else were you supposed to do?" Raul shook him slightly. "C'mon. There's got to be more."

"No! I swear!" Beads of sweat broke out on the man's greasy face, dotting his skin with marks of fear. "Nothing more. That's it."

Raul put his thumb on the hammer of the pistol

and pulled it back. The sound was loud in the tiny room, and the threat produced instant results.

"I gave him the name of some friends!" he cried. His voice shook, rising and falling in panic. "He needed more men. I told him who to call."

"Why did he need them?"

"I don't know!"

Tightening his hold on the drunk's collar, Raul pressed the muzzle of the pistol into the man's cheek; the pointed sight at the tip disappeared into the folds of his whiskered skin. "Don't make me repeat myself a third time. Why did he need more men?"

"I...I don't know, *señor*, truly!" The man was so full of dread he was quivering. "He didn't tell me."

"What kind of friends are these?"

The drunk blinked rapidly, then, obviously reading something in Raul's eyes, he spoke again, this time without any prompting. "Th-they're in the Army," he stuttered. "They have cars...and guns. He didn't tell me why he wanted them. He just said he needed some men who could get things done. I took him to their club and then I left. I swear."

"When did this happen?"

"Last night."

Raul nodded, then he pushed the man toward the door. He stumbled against the nearest wall, reached out and grabbed a cloudy mirror in a useless attempt to steady himself. It crashed to the floor, but neither of them looked. In the dark, tiny room, Raul could smell the man's fear, and he smiled in satisfaction. He'd use it, just like he used everything.

"We're going for a ride, and you're going to introduce me to your friends." Raul waved the gun toward the door. The man needed no more prompting.

Fifteen minutes later, they pulled up outside a building downtown. It looked dark and unoccupied, but as they waited, parked across the street in the SUV, Raul saw men coming and going through a door in the back corner, the only part of the building that seemed in use. Almost all of them wore uniforms and the standard look of arrogance and boredom South American officials favored, as they entered the private *choperia,* a club where the men could go and get their beer on tap, and on credit, too. The places were on every corner in Santa Cruz, but this one was obviously the sole domain of the men inside. He'd be crazy to try to enter it—and probably dead before his foot was in the door.

The drunk began to squirm, and Raul knew he had to do something with him. He couldn't turn him loose—he'd head straight for Kelman or his buddies inside the *choperia*—but Raul didn't want to kill him, either. As if he could sense Raul's dilemma, the man looked across the cab at his captor. Above the tape Raul had placed over his mouth, his bloodshot eyes were terrified.

Raul leaned over. "The men you introduced to Kelman—you sure they're here?"

The drunk nodded frantically.

"If you aren't sure, tell me now and save us both some grief."

The man couldn't talk, but he didn't need to. His eyes and his panicked nodding told Raul what he needed to know.

"All right," Raul answered. "We're going to sit here until they come out. Then you're going to tell me which one the *jefe* is. We're going to follow him and he's going to talk to me. Then you'll forget you ever saw me." He narrowed his gaze and patted the pistol he'd stuck in the waistband of his jeans. "If you lie to me, you'll regret it—but you won't care for too long. *¿Comprende?*" He waited for his words to soak into the man's pickled brain, then the nodding started again.

They settled in to wait.

AMAZINGLY, SHE SLEPT.

There was nothing else she could do, and after a while, Emma began to wonder how much was actually happening and how much she was dreaming. It didn't seem possible that only hours before she'd been in Raul's arms in Samaipata. The warmth of his embrace, the gentle kisses he'd given her, the hours of lovemaking in the old abbey—had they really happened, or was the harsh floor where she now huddled in fear the dream? She hadn't had an opportunity to grab her watch, so she had no idea how many hours had passed. Time blurred and so did her thinking.

At one point, she even imagined herself back home. She felt the tiny hands of her children on her face, their touch sweet and fleeting against her skin. The smell of baby powder hung in the air, along with the cry of the mockingbirds that nested by the nursery windows every year. She whispered their names. ''Sarah? Jake?''

But no one answered.

She thought then of the bag the men had found. She had no idea what had been in it or how it'd gotten there. A point of trivia popped into her discombobulated brain: Bolivia was the world's third-largest cultivator of coca. She'd seen the green leafy plants herself, growing on the mountain sides on the way to Samaipata. A certain amount was allowed each person. The locals drank tea made from the leaves and chewed them on occasion, sometimes using it in ceremonies. The *cocaleros* who grew more turned the plant into black paste, then shipped it to Colombia to be refined. Powdered cocaine was as illegal here as it was in the

States, but there was one difference: it wasn't often found inside the country. How had it gotten inside her house?

The drum of boots on the tile floor in the corridor outside finally broke her reverie. She jerked into awareness, every hair on her neck standing up, every nerve in her body quivering. She'd spent what seemed like forever listening for a sound—any sound—but nothing had happened. Now, as the noise replaced the silence, she longed for the quiet once more.

They were coming for her.

She leaped to her feet, then almost fell, her legs numb from sitting on the concrete floor, her back and shoulder stabbed with pain. She caught her balance and brought herself upright, just as the key rasped in the lock.

The scarred door flew open a second later. Emma's mouth fell open when she saw the man who stood on the threshold.

CHAPTER FOURTEEN

WILLIAM KELMAN'S blue eyes took in Emma's confusion. "Ms. Toussaint." His voice sounded concerned, caring. "Are you all right? You haven't been hurt, have you?"

She ignored his inquiry and stared at him, her initial shock changing quickly into suspicion. "Wh-what are you doing here? How did you find—"

He waved off her questions. "Not now," he said. "Let's get you out of here and then we'll talk."

She watched in amazement as the man who'd arrested her the night before came into the room. With quick, efficient movements, he turned her around, unlocked the handcuffs, then left. Following the cop out into the hallway, Kelman stopped when he saw that Emma wasn't behind him. She still stood in the center of the room, rubbing her chafed and bloody wrists, dazed by Kelman's appearance. He had to still be connected with the DEA, Emma thought with disconcertment. There was no other way he could have known about her nightmare—unless he had a darker connection to it. She wondered about this briefly, then she shut down her mind. She had to.

"Ms. Toussaint...are you coming?"

Emma shuffled forward, Kelman putting his hand under her elbow solicitously as he guided her down the corridor. Twenty minutes later, they were on her street, where Kelman parked his Jeep. She glanced at the clock on the dash and was shocked to read its face.

She'd been gone three hours.

She'd been gone a lifetime.

Kelman followed her to the front door and they both entered the foyer. The house felt different to Emma; something had seeped into the walls. Except for a few broken items here and there, the house looked the same as it had before, but it *wasn't* the same. Just like her, she thought through the blur of her incredulousness.

Walking slowly, she crossed into the living room. Two lamps gave off light, soft and faint. It painted the room with a deceptive order, washing the destruction of a nearby vase with a gentle touch. She looked around as if she didn't know quite where she was.

She shook her head and turned to Kelman. "They said I had drugs here. They found something—a bag—in the kitchen, but I have no idea what it was or how it got there. I...I don't know what's going on. I don't understand.''

Kelman walked over and picked up a pillow from the floor. He placed it on her sofa, then turned and fixed her with his eyes. Something in their blueness looked strange and out of place. Even in her confusion, she saw it and stilled, her pulse trapped inside her chest, fluttering like a wild bird. The feeling that she needed Raul came upon her unexpectedly. Immediately. Her eyes darted to the table where the phone usually sat, but it was gone. Then she remembered. She'd taken it upstairs when she'd tried to call him before. The handset was nestled in a pile of clothing at the bottom of her closet.

''You don't understand?'' He mocked her trembling voice—or was she imagining it? ''Then let me explain.'' He sat down and waved casually at one of her chairs, as if *he* lived here instead of her. ''Sit down, Emma, and I'll clarify it for you.''

She stood stiffly where she was.

''All right,'' he said, ''don't sit.'' His eyes hardened. ''But I do suggest you listen.''

She gripped the back of the chair nearest her, her legs turning weak at his tone. As he spoke again, a vision came to her: two suitcases filled with money and stock certificates, sitting in the vault at the bank. She'd thought she was past the point of being scared, but a trickle of fear managed to find its way into her frozen brain.

"I offered you the opportunity of a lifetime not too long ago. There was money to be made, but you turned it down. Do you remember?" His fingers curled on the arm of the sofa.

"I remember." Her voice was faint, as indistinct as the morning light.

"You understood what I was suggesting, didn't you, Emma? You're a very bright woman. I can't imagine you didn't."

"I wasn't sure," she answered.

"All I needed was some information," he said. "That's all. We could have both made more money than either of us will ever need, but you wouldn't cooperate."

"I couldn't." Trembling, but trying to hide it, she stared at him. "I can't break the law."

"You can't break the law?" He laughed lightly. "Then I'd say you have a problem. Because hiding a kilo of powdered coca is definitely breaking the law."

The part of her that was still alive screamed for her to run. But her feet stayed anchored to the floor, the twin forces of comprehension and horror pinning her to the spot.

She spoke quietly. "How did you know it was a kilo?"

"I weighed it." He smiled. "Right before I came in here and put it in your kitchen cabinet."

THEY WAITED three hours. The drunk sat in stupefied silence, his bleary eyes staring through the darkness. Every time a man came out of the *choperia,* he would sit up straighter and look harder. Raul had to give him credit for trying, but his friends weren't present. Obviously they'd left earlier, or they'd never been there at all. Dawn was breaking when a few stumbling patrons came out and the owner locked up.

Raul didn't doubt his captive. A .38 pointed at your gut for three hours was a strong incentive for telling the truth.

"All right." Raul spoke wearily and rubbed his stubbled chin. The rasping sound filled the truck. "That's it. We'll have to do it the hard way and go to his house, instead of catching him on the street. You're showing me where this guy lives, and we'll take it from there. One way or another, I'm finding out what's going on."

The man shook his head violently, and finally Raul was forced to pull the tape off. "What?"

"I don't know where he lives," the man gasped. His tongue snaked out and moistened his tortured lips. "I don't know, I swear. I just see him here, that's it."

The wave of exhaustion Raul had been fighting

crashed over him. He couldn't stay awake forever, and even if he did find the son of a bitch, who knew if Kelman had given him his orders yet? Raul had a bad feeling that time was running out, but there was nothing he could do about it right now.

It was almost five by the time they got back to the barrio. Raul cut the tape from the man's wrists and said, as he raised the gun, "This is simple." The weapon felt molded to his hand he'd held it so long. "You tell. You die. Understand?"

"Sí, sí, señor."

"I know where you live. I can come back. Anytime." He waited. "You think about that tonight when you go to sleep." The man nodded, and Raul waved the gun toward the door. "Get out."

The man scrambled out and ran toward his house. Putting the truck in gear, Raul drove slowly down the potholed street and headed for the First Ring. As he entered the traffic circle, he thought briefly of going to Emma's, but then reconsidered. She'd be getting ready for work and didn't need him around. He needed to clean up, too. He was soaked by the fumes that had wafted off the drunk in the close confines of the truck. He changed lanes and headed for home.

"WHY?" EMMA STARED at Kelman, the one word all she could get out.

"That's what I asked myself, too. Why? If you'd

helped me out the first time, then I wouldn't have had to resort to this. You wouldn't cooperate, though. So this is Plan B.''

She closed her eyes for a second. ''What do you want?'' she asked numbly.

''I want the rate,'' he answered. ''Currency trading is easy money—if you know which way to go. I'm tired of working hard for everything I've got.'' His eyes heated until they looked like two blue flames. ''Who do you think made the most money where I worked? The DEA agents who put their lives on the line or the *narcotraficantes?*'' He gave the word its proper Spanish pronunciation, and she realized at once he spoke Spanish. Perfect Spanish. He shook his head and answered his own question. ''The bad guys win, Ms. Toussaint. Or at least they did until they met me. Then they began to see the error of their ways. When they shared their route, I looked the other way. You didn't really think I made all that money working for the government, did you?''

''It wasn't any of my business how you made it.''

''That's right,'' he shot back. ''You were too busy thinking about how you could use it yourself, weren't you?'' He smiled. ''I saw the look in your eyes. You're as greedy as the rest of us.''

She couldn't deny the truth. Emma swallowed,

her whole body tight with fear. "But I turned you down."

"And now I'm giving you a second chance. This will be the last one, though. You don't get to pass *Go* a third time." He leaned forward and stared at her. "The government committee meets next week. You're going to find out which direction the *boliviano* is headed. Then you're going to make sure my money goes with it."

Her stomach knotted. "But why do you need to do this?" she asked desperately. "You have so much money already—"

"That's not the point," he said bluntly. "I need that cash cleaned. I'm in a new business venture with my local friends, and we want it washed. Trading it is the best possible way."

"It'll never work."

His eyes locked on hers. "Yes, it will. *You*'ll make it work."

"I can't."

"You can't, or you won't?" He shook his head. "If I were you, I'd think carefully about my answer. Whose blood do you want on your hands? Your own—or someone else's?"

She felt the color drain from her face. It took the last of her strength with it. "What do you mean?"

"I planted that bag of drugs when you and your lover were stranded in Samaipata. Did you think it was just bad luck your truck broke down? I planted the drugs, and I hired the men who came here to find them. I can arrange for it to happen again, too, but next time, it'll be for real. The men in the green uniforms who knock on your door will be genuine Bolivian cops—not military trash with bribes in their pockets.''

He waited a minute for her reaction, then continued, almost carelessly, ''If you don't believe me, I can give you another demonstration. We'll use Mr. Santos and see what happens.''

''Leave him out of this,'' she said quickly. ''He doesn't have anything to do with—''

''He doesn't?'' Nodding thoughtfully, Kelman paused for a second. ''Oh, right. Well, how about this, instead?''

He straightened one leg and reached into his back pocket. Emma wasn't sure what he was reaching for; she waited, her lungs still, her pulse roaring. When he brought his hand around, he held a square of paper.

''How about this?'' he said, holding it out to her. ''Will this change your mind?''

She didn't want to get any closer to him, yet her feet moved forward, bringing her toward the couch where he sat. With trembling fingers, she reached out and took the paper from his hand. It was a photograph.

Of Sarah and Jake.

The buzz in her ears stopped instantly; it had to, because her heart quit beating, the blood in her veins freezing into lines of solid horror. She stared at their innocent faces, then glanced at the date in the corner. It'd been taken two days before.

She raised her terrified eyes. "Where did you get this?" she asked hoarsely.

"It's a good picture, isn't it?" He nodded. "He's clever with a camera, but he's a very talented fellow. He can shoot with a lot of different things."

Emma sat down, her legs giving out entirely. It was only luck that there was a chair behind her. It rocked slightly as it took her weight, then settled back into the carpet. But her world continued to move. An emotional earthquake, she thought stupidly. Half the landscape was gone, and the rest would fall in the aftershocks to come.

"I can call my man and tell him to *shoot* some more if you need the time."

His choice of words was no mistake. All the panic, all the fear, all the disbelief she'd experienced in the past few hours crystallized instantly. Into something much different. She waited a beat, then raised her eyes to his. "You go near these kids and I'll kill you. That's a promise."

He smiled. "Does this mean we have a deal?"

WHEN THE DOOR closed behind Kelman, Emma went woodenly into the living room. She straightened the cushions on the couch and picked up the crystal shards, restoring some kind of order to the room but not to her brain. Then she went upstairs. Scrubbing her skin until it burned, she showered and shampooed her hair, dressing, when she was finished, in a terry-cloth warm-up. It was well over ninety degrees outside, but she couldn't stop shivering. With her hair wet and hanging down her back, she went downstairs.

Once in the kitchen, though, she stared blankly at the mess the men had left, her mind as void of thought as it'd ever been. She had no idea what to do next, where to even begin, but the first thing that came into her mind was Raul.

Then she remembered Kelman's threat. If she turned to Raul, Kelman would kill him. Recalling Raul's warning about the kind of man Kelman was, something told her Kelman didn't need the excuse her betrayal would give him.

He *wanted* Raul dead.

Raul had told her as much in Samaipata. She'd been too wrapped up in what had happened between them to think clearly, though. She'd been a fool not to see it before. Now she understood. She could never go to Raul.

Somewhere in the middle of all this, he'd begun to mean more to her than he should. She couldn't say she loved him; she wouldn't allow herself that luxury, but he'd slipped into her life and turned it upside down. The dark eyes, the slow hands, the mouth that fit her own so well… She'd recognized a kindred spirit in him the minute their eyes had met. He'd suffered, just as she had, and she couldn't be the one to bring him even more pain. Not when he'd given her such pleasure. And if he did find out, something told her he'd go about righting the wrong, and Kelman would win. He would kill Raul for sure, and she'd have his death on her hands—and in her heart—forever.

She shuffled to the breakfast table and sat down heavily, a stream of other possibilities fighting their way into her consciousness.

She could go to the police. But that would be a mistake. As she'd told Raul only a few days before, there was so much corruption in Bolivia that most foreign companies couldn't even operate in the country. Executives were routinely warned by their companies about the problem. She'd get no help from the Bolivian police. Kelman was no fool, and she was sure he'd already paid them to ignore her if she called.

Chris? She immediately shook her head. No. Her boss would take one look at the briefcases in that vault, then start to scream. And he'd have every right. She should have told him the minute Kelman had approached her, but she'd been too concerned that he would believe she couldn't do her job.

Reina's face shot into Emma's brain. Was there

anything she could do? Emma turned the idea over, helplessly realizing her friend had no idea of the extent of Kelman's manipulations. She'd be devastated with guilt, for she was the one who'd brought him to Emma. If Reina knew the kind of hell he'd visited on her, she was so impulsive she was just as likely to do something dangerous as she was to help.

So who was left?

After a moment, Emma answered herself, her words ringing emptily in the silence. "No one," she said. "No one can help me."

The monkey next door called out, and Emma raised her gaze, blurry and unfocused, to the mess in front of her. Details finally began to register. Her Earl Grey tea bags, emptied from their box. The silverware she'd bought at the local department store scattered across the floor. The cabinet doors of the pantry, gaping open.

Her attention was caught by something inside the small cabinet. She found herself staring at it, then, rising slowly, she made her way closer.

It was a bottle of vodka.

Reaching out, she closed her fingers around the bottle's neck, bringing it out into the light. She had no idea how the liquor had gotten into her pantry, but as she studied its clarity in the sunshine, she ventured a guess. Kelman. He'd probably brought it in, along with the drugs.

Go ahead, a small voice inside her said. *You deserve it. It'll help.*

She slowly twisted off the top and brought the bottle to her nose. There was no odor, but closing her eyes, she took a deep whiff, anyway, and something did reach her nose.

It was the smell of temptation.

A montage of faces and feelings rushed over her. Raul and their lovemaking, his words tender and sweet, his eyes black and hot. Her children and their innocence. Todd. And finally...Kelman. The faces shimmered and merged together beneath her eyelids. She wanted to forget them all. It was too painful, the choices too hard. The liquor could take off the edge and blur the agony. She opened her eyes.

Emma stared at the vodka, then jerked the bottle to her mouth and let her tongue flick over the edge. The sharp, familiar bite registered with a jolt, a reaction that went way past the simple taste. She closed down her brain and tilted the bottle higher.

Then the doorbell rang.

RAUL PRESSED THE BELL again. He could hear it echoing inside the house, and he shook his head. He had no idea what he was doing there; he'd gone home, cleaned up, then gotten in the truck and driven back to Emma's side of town. During the entire trip over, he'd told himself he was being ridiculous, but he couldn't get her out of his mind.

If he'd been someone else, he might have thought she was calling to him, using some kind of ESP. He didn't believe in that kind of nonsense, though.

He started to ring the bell again, then stopped when he heard the sound of a door closing inside the house. She was obviously at home. Why didn't she come to the front? He waited another few seconds, a concern he couldn't ignore growing inside him. Something was wrong.

He couldn't justify the feeling, but he didn't really care. Moving toward the window that faced her living room, he decided to break in. To hell with logic. But just as he raised a hand to test the glass, Emma appeared at the window beside the door.

At least, he thought it was her. The hollow-eyed, shell-shocked woman bore little resemblance to the woman whose bed he'd left almost six hours before, her skin warm from his touch, her eyes languid and full. She wore a heavy warm-up suit, and her face above the turned-up collar was pale and frightened, scrubbed of all makeup, her only color, as always, her full, red lips. Her wet hair hung in silken strands, framing her apprehensive expression. The transformation would have been unbelievable if the results weren't standing before him.

Blinking hard, she opened the door a scant two inches.

"My God, Emma!" he said. "What's wrong?"

"I...I think I must have caught what Reina had.

Y-you shouldn't come in." Her eyes were streaked with red, their hazel depths cloudy.

"It doesn't matter. Let me in. I can help you—"

"No!" She spoke quickly, the word coming out too strongly for someone ill. "I...I don't need anything, thanks, anyway. I...like to be alone when I'm not feeling well." She smiled wanly. "I'm not a good patient."

He looked into her eyes and could tell she was lying. She met his gaze, then looked away. She knew he knew. He felt the air leave his lungs, his heart squeezing into a ball of fear.

Kelman.

He'd sprung his trap and Emma had been caught. She wore the sick, helpless look of a wounded animal with no way out. The same look Raul had worn when Kelman had ambushed him.

"Emma?" He said her name softly. "What's going on? Tell me."

She started to shut the door, but she was too slow, her reflexes dulled by whatever had happened. His hand shot out, and he grabbed the mahogany, his fingers wrapping around the hard wooden edge.

She tried to push the door closed, but Raul forced his way inside, into the entry. She cried out, then stepped back, obviously choosing to give up as he slammed the door behind him. "Tell me what's going on," he demanded. "It's Kelman, isn't it? He's done something."

"I don't know what you're talking about." Her voice was harsh and painful. "And I don't appreciate the way you just barged in here, either. Please leave, Raul. Right now."

"I'm not going anywhere," he answered. "Not until you tell me the truth."

"I...I don't have anything to tell you." Blinking rapidly, she compressed her lips and brought her hands to her throat to pull the edges of her collar closer.

That's when he saw her wrists. They were scraped and raw, scarlet with scratches.

His stomach turned over, and he reached out and grabbed her forearms, raising them to eye level. She flinched, but he didn't release her. "Nothing happened? Then how do you explain *this?*"

She stared at him, a stubborn determination coming into her eyes, alongside the pain. She wasn't going to give away her secrets; she'd die before she did. That was when he understood what it would take to get her to talk. It was the last thing he wanted to do; it meant not just the sacrifice of everything between them but of his one and only goal, as well. But it was the only thing that would work.

He'd have to tell her the truth.

CHAPTER FIFTEEN

RAUL DROPPED her arms so abruptly Emma almost lost her balance. He turned and walked into the living room before she could stop him.

"Don't do this. I don't want you here." Following him into the room, she spoke, the lie sticking in her throat. She didn't know how, but she managed to say it without choking. She had to; Raul's very existence depended on it.

"I know that's what you want." Halting in the center of the room, he radiated pent-up energy. "But it's not going to happen until I say what I have to. I'm going to tell you why I'm here, what I'm doing, and how ruthless this man is. When I'm finished, you're going to hate me, but at least you'll understand. And maybe, just maybe, if you're lucky, you'll survive this."

She stared at him, her heart thumping. "What makes you so sure William Kelman's my problem? I could have a situation at work, or my kids could be in trouble, or..." She threw her hands up in the air. "Anything could be going on with me. Why do you think—"

"I don't have to think. I know. I know because he ruined my life." His pronouncement was flat, totally without emotion. "I spent five years in a federal prison because of William Kelman."

The words fell like stones at her feet. She felt faint, and for a moment she thought she'd throw up. "Wh—what are you saying?" she asked. "I don't understand."

"He destroyed my life over a woman. And I didn't even love her. Not like I love—" He broke off abruptly and shook his head, a gesture filled with regret and something else, something that darkened his eyes to a shade she'd never seen before.

"Her name was Denise Murphy, and she came up to me in a D.C. bar. I'd just ended a relationship with someone else, and I wasn't at my best. Denise said she'd seen me around town and wondered who I was." He shrugged. "She was gorgeous— a tall brunette with a perfect body—and I took her home with me that night. It was the biggest mistake I ever made."

Emma's nausea grew. It took up all the space inside her and forced its way up into her throat.

"Denise Murphy was living with William Kelman at the time, but she was looking for a way out. I provided her with the excuse. She left him and we had a brief affair. I didn't know all this until she visited me in prison to explain."

"To explain? Explain what?"

"Kelman ruled the local DEA office like he was some kind of king. He was making a fortune by working *with* the dealers, tipping off the agents on the minor ones and taking payoffs from the big ones when the raids went down. His bosses had no idea what he was doing. Denise only knew because she lived with him.

"She said he hadn't always been that way, but his wife had left him a few years before, and it seemed to push him over the edge." Raul paused for a second, then continued, "When Denise did the same thing—left him—he saw himself as a two-time loser. He couldn't believe it'd happened again, so he took care of it."

"Took care of it?"

Raul nodded. "He planted drugs and a gun in my car while I was out of town. I was stopped, and the rest, as they say, is history."

She had a vague understanding of how Kelman had arranged things here, but how could he do the same thing in the States? It didn't seem possible. "But how did he get the officer to stop you?"

"He was told to by a DEA agent. Kelman had something on the agent, and offered to let the guy off the hook if he took me down. All the cop had to do was catch me in a traffic violation—I turned right without signaling. That gave him cause to pull me over, and he held me till the DEA agents got there—they were in it, as well. They asked if they could search the car, and I had no reason to refuse. One of them opened up the trunk and pulled out a plastic bag of coke I'd never seen before. And a nickel-plated .45.''

"Kelman planted them," she said faintly.

He nodded. "I'd left my car at the airport and flown to the Bahamas for a weekend. He did it while I was gone.''

"But five years. My God, why so long? Did he own the judge, too?''

"He didn't have to. There are guideline sentences for drug violations in the federal system. Whatever number of years you're sentenced, you serve eighty-five percent of it, regardless. I was a first-time offender, but it didn't matter. Nothing mattered. The evidence couldn't be disputed, and I was tried and convicted in very short order. I was sent to Cumberland, Maryland.'' In a hard tone he spoke again. "I lost my home, my savings and my license to practice law. Everything.''

His voice held no emotion, but Emma could see his pain, smell it, even taste it. She hadn't moved since he'd begun to speak, and now she walked away from him. She had to put some space between them, had to escape the agony she knew he felt. Crossing the room, she stood in front of the window that looked out on her garden. The walled area was serene and quiet in the morning sun, a total contrast to the chaos raging inside her.

She let it storm, giving no hint of how she felt. After a few minutes, through the confusion, a thread of understanding began to take form. He'd had everything that was important to him taken away—just as she had. From a woman's point of view, nothing meant more to her than her children, but a man's priorities were different, especially a man who didn't have a family. He judged himself by what he could do with his career, with his ability to make a living.

Kelman had taken away the very essence of who Raul was. And he'd replaced him with a far different man.

Emma turned slowly and looked at Raul. The planes of his face, the angles of his body, even the way he held himself—how different was he now? She could only imagine. Not understanding at the time, she'd sensed his former self, sensed a far different man when they'd made love and when they'd visited the orphanage, but the core of who he was no longer existed. It'd been changed forever, *lost* forever.

Except for one detail.

His determination.

The realization didn't come to her in a flash. It wasn't like the movies where all at once the heroine understood. This was completely different.

The truth formed itself slowly and opened up only after she examined it closer. He waited patiently, as if he understood what she was dealing with, then finally, when the thought was fully constructed from the pieces he had given her, she spoke. Carefully. Slowly.

"You came to Santa Cruz *because* of Kelman. You followed him down here."

"That's right."

"And the money in your account…"

"It's from a slush fund the State Department manages. The woman who was with me at Candelabra arranged it. She's…an old friend."

Dust motes danced in the tense silence between them. "You're not an importer."

"No. I'm not an importer."

"You have no business here, other than tracking down Kelman?"

"That's right. Denise knew he would come here, and Wendy told me when he arrived. She had the passports checked."

Emma looked at him, her heart locking into place with a click. She knew the answer to the question, but she had to ask it, anyway. She had to hear his reply. "And my role in all this is…?"

"I came here to stop him. And to do that, I had to get next to the person he'd need the most. That was you."

Her heart kept beating, her lungs kept working,

her brain kept going, but something inside Emma died. She actually felt the passing and mourned the emotion before she knew what it was.

After another moment, she understood what was leaving her; it was the hope she'd had, the hope she hadn't even been able to acknowledge until now, that they might have some kind of future together. That Raul might say, "I love you," and she would say the same thing. That he'd help her get her children and they might be a family. That her life might start again. All those possibilities were gone forever now.

Raul's voice reached her through a fog. "Kelman didn't pick Reina out of the blue to be his real-estate agent, Emma. He chose her because he knew she was friends with you. He knew when he said he needed a banker, she'd arrange an introduction. He manipulated the situation to get what he wanted—you—just like he always does." Raul paused as if to gather himself. "You're the best banker in town, Emma. He knew to come to you. All I had to do was watch and wait."

"You son of a bitch." Lifting her head, she spoke quietly, the fury behind her words almost anticlimactic. "You acted as if you cared for me, and all along you knew he was going to destroy me! How could I have been so dumb?"

"I didn't act *as if* I cared for you. I *do* care for you," he said softly. "More than you know. And

I wasn't going to let him destroy you. I did everything I could to protect you. I would have done
more if you'd told me what was going on. Please,
Emma..." He took a step in her direction, then
stopped when she held up her hand.

"No. No." She laughed softly, a bitter sound
that echoed in the tension-filled room. "Don't tell
me that now. Not now. I might fall for it once, but
twice? No way. I'm not that stupid."

"None of this is important right now," he said,
interrupting her. "All that matters is stopping Kelman."

She held up her hand again, an angry flush burn-
ing its way into her cheeks. "Are you crazy? He's
threatened my children! Do you know what that
means? Do you have any idea?"

"Whatever he's done to you, Emma, I promise
I'll make him pay for it. I promise."

"You promise!" She mocked his words then
shook her head in disgust. "My God. I *trusted* you.
With my body, with my secrets, with my heart.
You wooed me. You told me to believe in you and
I did."

"I didn't know you at that point. You were a
stranger and I didn't care. But now I do." His jaw
tightened. "Let me help you, Emma. If we work
together, we can stop him."

The decision was an easy one. She looked him
straight in the eye. "I don't trust you. I'd never

ask for your help.'' She held up her hand again to stop him from speaking. ''I don't need it, either. *I'll* make William Kelman pay for what he's done by myself, like I've done everything else in my life. All I want from you is to leave. Right now.''

''I can't do that.''

''Oh, yes, you can.'' She pointed toward the entryway. ''You walk out of here, close the door behind you, and forget you ever knew me. It's easy.''

''It's *not* easy, and I wouldn't do it even if it was. Just let me help.''

She closed the space between them with two angry steps. Energy burned inside her and fueled her anger. She wanted to strike him, but it wouldn't have done any good. ''You're here to help yourself, Raul, and no one else. You don't give a damn about me and you never have. All you want is revenge.''

''Emma, please...''

Her heart split open, the pain too much for it to hold. She wheeled around and faced the window, her arms wrapped around herself as if to contain the agony. ''Get out,'' she said thickly, her back to him. ''And shut the door behind you.''

HE TOLD HIMSELF it didn't matter. Moving down Emma's walkway, Raul ignored the ache in his chest. All that was important was Kelman, he repeated. Nothing counted but him.

He passed through the broken gate, the words of staunch determination fueling his departure. If she wanted to fight the devil on her own, then by God, let her.

Raul would spend the rest of his life tracking down Kelman, and if he wasn't able to stop him here, then he'd stop him somewhere else. It didn't matter where. Raul wouldn't quit until he'd visited the same pain on Kelman that the other man had visited on him.

Emma Toussaint was disposable. When he'd used her up, Kelman would move on to his next victim, and she'd join the list of people he'd screwed. Raul couldn't care less.

Nothing mattered. She didn't matter, and everything they'd shared didn't matter. She'd been a chance he played, and it hadn't worked out. He strode down the sidewalk without looking right or left, his anger contained within the tiny kernel where he kept all the rest of his emotions.

By the time he climbed into the truck and started the engine, he knew how badly he was lying to himself. By the time he got to the end of the block, he knew he could go no farther.

He *did* care. He cared so much it scared the hell out of him. And he was a bigger bastard than he thought if he left Emma to face Kelman on her own.

Raul pulled up to the stop sign and sat, the truck idling beneath him in the hot sunlight. A sweep of anger came over him, a sweep so intense, so powerful, that it blinded him, and he began to pound the steering wheel in frustration.

It was happening all over again! Kelman was taking away the only thing Raul cared about.

The warm hazel eyes, the silky blond hair, the skin so soft and tender. Couldn't Kelman see what kind of woman Emma was? Didn't he know how much her kids meant to her? Or her job, her friends? She was the woman every man spent his life searching for, and she deserved much more than she'd gotten so far. If Raul had had half an idea of the kind of woman she was, he would never—*never*—have let this happen as he had. He hadn't known, though. Now things were different.

He'd held her in his arms and made love to her. He knew who she was and what she represented. And it was up to him to keep her safe from Kelman, even if she didn't want his help. Even if she hated him and never wanted to see him again.

He loved her, he realized with a jolt. And love meant so much more than revenge....

EMMA WENT UPSTAIRS and straight to her desk. Raul's revelation had sliced her like a razor, but the fierce pain brought with it a sudden clarity. She knew exactly what she had to do. She couldn't allow herself to think about anything else, but most of all she couldn't think about the fact that she'd let him into her heart when he'd only been using her. She simply couldn't face it. Not now.

She picked up the phone and punched out the numbers to bring up an overseas line. When she heard the familiar buzz, she dialed the rest of the digits. Todd answered almost immediately.

"I've got something to tell you." She spoke with no preliminary when he said hello. "Don't ask any questions—just listen to me carefully and do exactly what I say."

He sputtered something, but she ignored it. "I'm in trouble down here. There's a man who's trying to blackmail me, and he knows about you and the children. You have to take Sarah and Jake away from there. Today."

As she gave voice to the words, the enormity of what she was doing hit her. She should have been crying, should have been hysterical, but there were no more tears and no more emotions left in her heart. She'd just handed Todd a loaded gun and pointed it at her head.

To protect her children, she had to destroy any chance she might have in the future of getting them back.

"What kinda crap are you pulling now?"

She cut through his drawl. "I'm serious, Todd. This guy is for real, and he's dangerous. He has photos of the kids, photos he had taken this week. I want you to leave and get them somewhere safe." Her heart cramped. "I don't want to know where you're going, either. I...I can't know."

"Are you drinkin' again, Emma Lou? This is crazy talk!"

"I'm telling you the truth! The kids are in danger. You have to leave, Todd."

"What'd you do?"

She started to explain, then stopped. He'd never believe her, and what did it matter, anyway? "I didn't do anything, but it's not important," she said. "Nothing is but getting those kids hidden, okay?"

"Emma, honey, get a grip. We can't just up and leave here. Jake's got a ridin' lesson this afternoon, and Sarah's goin' to a birthday party...."

"Todd." Emma said his name, then waited until he stopped talking. "I am *not* crazy. I am *not* kidding. And I am definitely *not* drunk. If you don't believe me, then you're putting yourself and the children in jeopardy." Understanding she'd have to tell him more to get him to comply, she explained what Kelman wanted as quickly as possible. "This guy is ex-DEA, and he knows how to work the system," she said when she'd finished. "He'll make it look like an accident, but something will happen, okay? Something very bad. Believe me—I've had a taste of it already, and you do not want to go through that.''

In a subdued voice, Todd asked her several more questions, and she answered them, praying the whole time he would believe her. Finally she heard his chair squeak as he tilted it upright—a sure sign he was beginning to take her seriously.

''Why don't you just call the police?''

''That's not how it works down here.''

''Well, there's got to be someone who could help you. Your boss, a friend…somebody, surely.''

Raul's black gaze flashed in front of Emma's face, but she closed her eyes—and her heart. ''There's no one,'' she answered. ''I'm in this alone. I can handle it, though, if I know the kids are safe. That's all I care about.''

He didn't speak; he was thinking about it, she realized. She pushed him. ''It won't be for long. The committee meets next week. I can have everything in place by then.''

''What are you going to do?''

She lied. ''I'm not sure yet, but I can't do anything unless Sarah and Jake are hidden. I have to know they're all right.''

''I guess Mother would take them for a while—''

''No! Not there!'' Todd's parents were very

well-known, their bayou house, Belle Rive, a showcase. Kelman's man could ask anyone in town, and they'd point the way—or even worse, take him straight to the place. Emma gripped the edge of her desk. "He could find them there, Todd. That's too easy. You'll have to hide them. You'll have to take them somewhere unexpected."

"But Belle Rive has great security! No one can get through those gates—"

"Todd. Todd! You aren't listening to me. This man has people who can do anything. He's got cops in his pocket, okay? The children would not be safe at Belle Rive. Trust me on that."

Another pause, this one longer, then he spoke. "Well, then how about the place where—"

"Don't tell me," she interrupted, the shreds of what was left of her heart turning to ashes. "I don't want to know, okay? It's better that way. Just make sure it's safe—really safe—then take them and hide them. If everything works out, I'll call you when it's over. If I don't call…well, I guess you'll figure it out."

"Emma, I…I don't know what to say. Isn't there anything I can do to help you?"

For a second, his offer sounded genuine, and she wanted to believe him, wanted to desperately. Then she realized he wasn't the man she wanted to believe in. She wanted to hear those words—and trust them—from Raul.

She shook her head and closed her throat to the tears that were building inside. "There's only one thing you can do," she answered thickly. "Kiss the kids for me and tell them I love them."

CHAPTER SIXTEEN

THE NEXT WEEK was torture. Every time the phone rang, every time her office door opened, every time Emma saw a gray-haired man walking down the sidewalk, she'd go weak. She stopped eating and stopped sleeping. By Friday morning, she'd aged five years and lost ten pounds.

The currency committee met early. As the clock struck ten, the report was delivered to the bank, the new rate set and ready to be announced. She waited for Chris to step away from his desk and head for the men's room as he did every day before lunch, then Emma slipped into his office. With trembling fingers, she picked up the committee's bulletin and scanned it rapidly.

It should have been harder, she thought, returning to her own office several minutes later. Breaking the law, ruining her life, giving up everything she'd worked for the past two-plus years, should have been more difficult. With just a few keystrokes, though, it was all over, the irrevocable plan set into motion as she deposited Kelman's money into an open account.

The enormity of her actions soaked in a few minutes later. She raced to the bathroom and threw up the only thing she'd put in her stomach for days—the cup of tea she'd had for breakfast—retching and coughing until there was nothing left inside her. Sitting weakly on the floor of the bathroom, she rested her forehead against the cold porcelain edge of the toilet. Needing more strength than she would have ever dreamed necessary, she finally rose up and staggered to the basin.

She looked worse than the Quechua on the corner, she thought, staring in the bathroom mirror. Who was the tormented woman reflected in the glass, her eyes so empty and flat?

Emma turned away from the reflection and began to scrub her hands. She couldn't wash away her thoughts, though. Reaching for a towel, she dried her fingers and brought the damp cloth to her forehead, patting it feebly.

She'd just sacrificed her future to keep her children safe. It was the ultimate irony, she thought, shaking her head. To protect them, she'd had to give away any chance she'd ever have to be with them again. To have a normal life, to be their mother. She'd flushed it all away, and no one would ever understand why. No one but Raul.

She gripped the edge of the counter and swayed slightly. His life was at stake, too, and even though she knew she should hate him for what he'd done, she couldn't. She actually understood. But that didn't mean she could forgive him. He'd used her and nothing would ever make that right.

Nothing.

She made one more swipe across her face with the towel, then dropped it on the counter and reached into her pocket for the tube of lipstick she'd brought with her. The slash of color she applied to her lips looked garish and overdone under the harsh fluorescence. She wiped some of it off, then tried again, but the result was the same. A made-up corpse would have looked better.

What did it matter? She left the bathroom, thinking the look was actually pretty appropriate. After all, that was what she was, wasn't she? A walking dead woman?

She went straight to her desk, collected her purse, then told Felicity she was leaving.

"See you Monday," the receptionist said.

Emma stared at the woman for a few seconds, then turned and walked out of the lobby without saying a word. *See you Monday?* She didn't think so.

In a nauseous daze, she flagged down the first cab she could. When she reached her house, she went inside and headed for the living room. She made only one stop—at the chest just inside the room. She opened the top drawer and reached inside, her shaking hands gripping the package she'd hidden there a few days before.

Taking the first chair she came to, she sat down to wait. It wouldn't take long, she was sure.

SLOUCHED BEHIND the wheel of a beat-up red Passport outside the bank, Raul straightened as he saw Emma leave. He glanced at his watch in surprise. It was early—barely lunchtime. Emma never left before six. Was it finally going down?

In the past week, he'd actually watched Emma fade. She'd lost a visible amount of weight, and the circles under her eyes had grown darker and darker. She looked like a ghost as she drifted down the sidewalk and held out her hand to hail a taxi. Her dark dress hung on her like a sack, and her skin had a greenish hue.

He hadn't tried to approach her. She'd made it more than clear that she didn't want him in her life, but that wasn't how it was going to end. He couldn't let it stop like that. Not after realizing that he loved her, even though he knew he shouldn't.

At first, he'd considered storming Kelman's house and confronting him—preferably with a loaded .45. After he'd calmed down, Raul had realized that kind of action would have been satisfying but useless. The man had put something into motion already, and if Raul killed him, who knew how it would end? He couldn't go to him now.

Instead, he'd stuck with Emma. Kelman would eventually show up, and if Raul stayed with her, he'd make sure she was safe.

She wasn't aware of it, but he'd known where she was and what she was doing since he'd left her house last week. He'd even slept in the car outside her house at night, changing the rentals every day so there'd be no chance she'd recognize the vehicle.

When Kelman came, Raul would be ready.

Raul put the SUV in gear and joined the flow of movement, heading away from the bank, to follow the path of her taxi. There was a lot of traffic on the street already, and he had trouble keeping the vehicle in view. A short time later, it headed toward her neighborhood, and he dropped back some more. She wouldn't recognize the rental he was driving, but the extra distance would make sure she didn't see him.

She climbed out of the cab as soon as it stopped, paying the driver through the window before she turned and headed up the sidewalk. Parking down the street, Raul watched her stride toward the gate, an empty feeling of loss echoing deep inside him.

Darkness came early, a spring storm brewing. Under the cover of the cloudy sky, Raul slipped from the truck an hour later, reaching the house of Emma's neighbor a few seconds after that. In the silence, he glanced around, then jumped straight up, his fingers barely making the edge of the tall, stuccoed wall. Scrambling over the top, he let go and fell into their yard, a hard thud accompanying his landing. He grunted, then rolled to his feet.

The people who lived in the house were gone; he'd seen them load their car the day before with enough suitcases to last a month. The live-in maid had waved goodbye, and two minutes after they'd driven away, she'd disappeared, as well. The house was empty.

Creeping through the heavy underbrush that lined the perimeter of the wall, Raul advanced stealthily to the rear of the garden. His plan was simple. Wait in Emma's yard. It was the only way he could see Kelman's arrival if he came in the back way—and he would. Kelman never approached anything head-on. The frustration Raul felt at not being able to do this sooner had been driving him crazy.

In the wall that separated the two houses, a series of decorative cutouts was carved, iron grillwork filling the spaces. Raul had seen the openings the night Emma had brought him into her backyard, but he hadn't realized until now how clearly they showed her whole house from this angle. Glancing over now through the one closest to the street, he could see straight into her living room. He stopped abruptly and stared.

She was sitting in the room.

His breathing rasped in the hushed humid air, the sound as rapid as his heartbeat. Emma looked like a statue in contrast, carved and cold. She sat immobile, her blinking eyes her only motion. In her lap, her fingers were knit together. She might have been holding something, but he really couldn't tell.

His throat burned, and all at once, he wanted to leap over the wall and tell her he was there and nothing could make him leave. He wanted to tell her he was sorry.

He wanted to tell her he loved her.

Lifting his hands, Raul wound his fingers in the lacy grillwork. The metal bars framed Emma, as if she was in a prison, and he shuddered as the idea burned into his brain.

A moment later, something heavy crashed into the side of his head. Raul collapsed into the grass, the night spinning around him.

THE MONKEY NEXT DOOR screamed, and Emma started, the heavy weapon almost rolling off her lap. She caught the gun at the last minute, her fingers closing around it reflexively, her nails digging into the rubber grip to leave half-moon marks of anxiousness. The animal frequently howled for no reason. As scary as the sound was, it signified nothing.

Telling herself to relax, she leaned back against

the chair, her shoulders stiff and tight. Rotating the muscles first one way and then the other, she started to take a deep breath, then she froze. There was someone in the hallway of her house. The muffled step and corresponding creak of the board resounded in Emma's heart. The monkey's cry had obscured his entrance. Her pulse faltered when she heard the sound again. It was louder this time.

She was out of her chair and standing when he stepped into the doorway. They stared at each other for five seconds, Kelman's eyes angry and cold, Emma matching his look, her determination fierce. He opened his mouth to speak, but she didn't wait.

She raised the gun and fired.

Incredibly, she missed. With the deafening sound of the shot still echoing around the room, Kelman recovered with a scream and lunged toward her. Before she could fire again, he was beside her. He grabbed the barrel of the gun and jerked it from her. A sickening wave of fear rolled over her as she felt the weapon leave her grasp.

"What in hell do you think you're doing?" He clutched the pistol, holding it out of her reach. "You damn near killed me!"

"That was my plan!" Her chest heaved, her breath coming fast. "Did you think I would let you blackmail me, threaten my children—ruin my life—and get away with it?"

"Ruin *your* life? What do you call what you've done to me?"

He was panting with the effort of disarming her, yet his glare was so cold, so chilling, she felt a shiver go up her back. If she'd needed any confirmation, this was it. He knew what she had done.

"I can't be responsible for changes in the market."

He shook his head like an angry bull. "The market didn't change. You deliberately traded that money the wrong way. You bought dollars, and you should have bought *bolivianos*. You knew what was going on, and you went the wrong way on purpose."

"Not according to the change order you signed. You *told* me to buy dollars. I have it in writing." She stared at him steadily, while inside she was quivering.

His eyes narrowed into two angry slits. "I didn't sign any such order and you know it."

"Maybe I do," she said slowly, "but no one else will. I *have* a signed order, and it's locked in my desk."

Her words took up all the space between them and filled the tense silence. After a moment, he shook his head, a gleam approaching admiration coming into his cold gaze.

"You planned this, didn't you? The trade, my anger...this." He lifted the gun, and the metal caught the light and glinted malevolently. "You were going to tell the police I was angry over the trade and broke in here. That you killed me in self-defense." He shook his head. "I'd almost be impressed, Emma, except it didn't quite pan out, did it?"

"The night's not over yet," she said.

"That's the first thing you've been right about all evening."

He smiled, and something skittered down her back again, something cold and truly fearful. Refusing to give him the pleasure of seeing her fright, Emma held herself stiff and gazed back.

"Let's go upstairs." He looked at the gun and tossed it onto the sofa, clearly having other plans. "It's time for this farce to end...."

HE WASN'T OUT but a second; the smell of dirt brought him quickly to his senses. Rolling over, then standing in one quick motion, Raul came up fighting, his fist connecting solidly with his very first punch.

A grunt sounded, then a *whoosh* of air flew by his jaw as a swing was delivered. It came a moment too late to land, and Raul ducked instinctively. He was fighting a shadow, but he didn't really care. Whoever it was, he meant to stop Raul, and Raul couldn't let that happen. He feinted left and struck right. Again the hit connected, and the

dark outline of a man pitched backward. Raul
threw himself on top of his attacker and struck out
blindly, his knuckles scraping over the thick
whiskered jaw time and time again. The man cried
out and raised his arms, but it was a useless attempt
to protect himself. Raul continued to pummel until
his fist gleamed wetly in the darkness and the other
man whimpered, curling into a ball in the grass at
his feet.

Raul pulled back, his chest heaving, his gasps
loud and painful in the pitch-black garden. He took
three deep breaths, then scrambled to his feet and
pulled the man up with him by his collar. Dragging
him to the front of the yard, Raul recognized him
instantly.

It was Kelman's drunk, the man who'd put the
bug in Emma's purse. Raul cursed soundly. "I
should have killed you when I had the chance."
He jerked the man around and started to pat him
down. In his pocket he found an ancient .38, a
replacement for the one Raul had taken from him
before. With another curse, Raul pulled the weapon
out and stuck it in the waistband of his pants.
"What in hell do you think you're doing?"

The minute his mind cleared, Raul understood,
not needing an answer to his question. Kelman had
brought the man with him as a precaution in case
someone unexpected showed up at Emma's. Some-

one like Raul. A flash of white rage swept through him as the implication sunk in.

The drunk read Raul's expression and his face collapsed with fear. He cried out and reached up to pry Raul's fingers from his shirt collar, but he wasn't fast enough.

Cocking his fist, Raul reared back then smashed his knuckles into the man's jaw, every ounce of force and rage he had stored up for Kelman behind the punch. It landed squarely with a loud crack, pain ricocheting up Raul's arm and into his shoulder. He never even noticed. Instantly the drunk's body went slack, and Raul let it drop like the useless bag of garbage it was. He never looked back as he ran.

KELMAN'S PRONOUNCEMENT took a moment to soak in. When it did, Emma started shaking her head and backing up. He took a step toward her and grabbed her by the elbow, his fingers biting into her flesh. He pulled her into the hall and said roughly, "You don't have a choice in this one. You've used up all your chances."

She struggled against him, kicking and lashing out, but it did no good. He was strong and he was angry. Hauling her toward the stairs, he started upward, and she had to follow or fall down and be dragged. They reached the top and he turned right to go into her bedroom. He pushed her into the room and slammed the door shut, a finality to the action that made her turn weak.

"Get in there," he said, tilting his head toward her bathroom.

Again, she didn't move, and this time when he grabbed her, he was even more violent. His fingers locked around her upper arm with a bruising force, and swearing loudly, he pushed her into the bathroom, throwing her to the hard marble floor once they stepped inside. She watched as he reached into his pocket.

When he yanked his hand back out, he held a small plastic bottle. He pitched it at her, and she raised her hands in defense, catching it at the very last minute.

It was a common medicine vial from the *farmacia* around the corner. Like all the pharmaceutical shops located on every street in Santa Cruz, you could walk in and buy any drug you wanted. Most required no prescription. The label was written in Spanish, but a single word leaped out to Emma's startled gaze. *Valium.*

From his coat pocket, he pulled out another bottle, and this one she recognized even before he tossed it to her. She dropped the pills into her lap and caught the bottle as it sailed toward her. It was a pint of vodka. She looked at him questioningly.

"You've been very depressed. Everyone at the office has noticed your weight loss, the bags under your eyes, the mistakes you've been making. They haven't known why, but tomorrow, when the police ask, they'll point out that you weren't looking well.''

His eyes glittered in the darkness and his voice went deeper. ''Your ex-husband will confirm everything. He knows how unstable you've been lately. The drugs and the alcohol won't surprise him a bit.'' Kelman shook his head. ''It'll be a shame, but everyone will understand since you had a little problem before. You didn't have a choice. You missed your children and hated your job. Your only answer was suicide.''

CHAPTER SEVENTEEN

ONCE THE SHOCK of his words wore off, a cold, stark image came to Emma, worming into her brain like some kind of insidious bug, tunneling its way in and bringing with it all the pain, all the horror, all the truth she'd been trying to escape. For a second, for just one single second, she actually thought she might agree. Everything *would* be over that way, wouldn't it? Facing the consequences of what she'd done here, facing the fact that she'd never have her children, even facing the truth of Raul's betrayal, it would all be in the past, part of her history.

She'd be dead; she wouldn't care.

Then she thought again, and the truth of what her death would really mean came to her. It would mean he won. And no one, except Raul, would know the truth. Within a very short time, he would probably be dead, too. Kelman would find a way to murder him, or almost worse, lock him up again, and then Kelman would be free to do whatever he wanted.

Suddenly she understood the depth of Raul's

commitment to this evil man's destruction. If she'd been Raul, she would have been equally committed. She would have used him just as he'd used her, if it meant stopping this man. She closed her eyes and forgave Raul, forgave him and accepted that she loved him—even though he'd never know that either.

"Drink up, Emma. Wash down the pills." Kelman spoke almost compassionately. "All of them."

She locked her eyes on his. "When hell freezes over."

He waited, as if thinking about what to do, then all at once, he was at her side. In a heartbeat, he had both bottles open and her jaw in his hand. Slapping his other hand over her nose, he cut off her breath. She lasted as long as she could, her vision growing dim, until nature took over and she opened her mouth to gasp in air. Instantly, he poured in the pills and liquor, then he snapped her mouth shut and held her face tight.

"Swallow," he said, all pretense gone. He shook her face. "Now!"

Choking and gagging, Emma tossed her head violently but after a few seconds, the inevitable happened. She swallowed. Then swallowed again. The vodka burned, the taste of it unbelievably strong as it mixed with the pills and began to dissolve them. He kept her jaws clamped together and she continued to fight. In a moment it was over and he released her.

Still on all fours and coughing uselessly, Emma scrambled to the opposite corner of the room, her breathing ragged and hoarse. She opened her mouth and tried to spit. There was nothing left, though. She'd swallowed all of it. She lifted her head, her stomach churning. She wanted to curse him, to scream, to attack him as she'd planned, but all she could do was stare at him blankly.

He crossed his arms and leaned against the wall with an air of casual calmness as he waited for her to die.

DESPITE EVERYTHING, some vestige of the man he'd once been still lived in Raul. He knew this was true because it'd never been his intention to kill Kelman. But as he leaped over the wall separating the two houses and sprinted for Emma's house, this last reminder of who he had been disappeared. Rage and pent-up frustration filled him, and he could think of only one thing: seeing Kelman dead. It was no longer enough to take his money or ruin his life. Raul wanted to kill him. Preferably with his bare hands.

The front door was locked. Cursing, Raul turned and ran to the back of the house. Someone had already jimmied open the door off the terrace. He stepped inside the house, his heart pounding loudly enough to reveal his presence, he was certain. He paused and forced himself to listen.

There was nothing but silence, then he heard conversation, faint but definitely there. He lifted his face to the ceiling and wished he could see through the rafters to the floor above. They were there, but where? And doing what? Did Kelman have a weapon?

It didn't really matter. Raul slipped through the house and made his way up the stairs, pulling the drunk's ancient pistol from the waistband of his pants. Holding his breath, he paused at the top, his hand on the doorknob. He turned it slowly, then exhaled a prayer of thanks when the knob gave way. He tensed, then threw open the door.

The room was empty.

But from the adjoining bathroom, the muted sound of voices could be heard. He crossed the bedroom, stopping once more when he reached the door to the bath. The sound of Kelman's smug voice, mixing with the low and pleading tones of Emma's, reached out and grabbed Raul. The sensation was physical; he felt it come under the door and jump up and choke him.

With his hand gripping the pistol, Raul put his shoulder to the door, twisted the knob and burst into the room.

EMMA SCREAMED as the door flew open, but it was a reflexive action borne of survival. Her body and mind had already started to shut down, the drugs beginning their work. Lying in the corner of the room, she fought to focus, blinking rapidly, but the man tumbling into the room moved too fast for her to follow. Even Kelman's voice, as he bellowed in surprise, came to her from a well. It was stretched out, too, like music played too slow, the name he uttered making no sense to her cloudy brain.

The two figures wrestled in the tiny confines of the bathroom, their curses and grunts signaling the violence of their fight. Emma commanded her legs and arms to lift her up and get her out of the hell she was in, but they wouldn't listen. It was all she could do to raise her head from the cold marble floor. A second later, the two men came crashing in her direction, locked together, rolling as one. She tried to escape the inevitable, but she simply couldn't move. The two heavy bodies collided with her limp one. She blinked and cried out, the knee of one of the men slamming into her stomach.

Her breath left her in a *whoosh,* and the jolt of it, the pain of it, cleared her mind, if only for a second. Raul came into focus. He was on top of Kelman, struggling to hold him down, a gun in his hand only inches from her face. She strained to figure out where the gun had come from—hadn't Kelman left it downstairs? Before she could reason it out, Raul lifted Kelman's wrist and smashed it into the marble, the sickening crunch of breaking bone sounding above their rasping breaths.

"Take the pistol," Raul screamed. "Take it, Emma! Take it and shoot him!"

Their eyes connected, but Emma could no more have seized the weapon than she could have fired it accurately. In another second, the two men rolled away from her. Instead of moving inches, they seemed to travel miles. Paralyzed, she watched them go, but before they did, she saw the expression in Raul's wild gaze. It was pure disbelief. He didn't understand why she refused to help. He didn't know it was because she couldn't. He believed it was because she wouldn't.

It was her final thought. Emma's eyes rolled back into her head and everything else disappeared.

EMMA'S REFUSAL stunned him, but his instincts kicked in and saved him from distraction. Raul pounded Kelman's hand once more into the marble, the pistol trapped between them, neither willing to release his grip. Raul should have shot him the minute he'd pushed open the door, but he'd been too startled once he'd seen Emma. Kelman had taken advantage of the moment and managed to grab the gun.

Kelman's knuckles were bloody and ragged, yet he continued to hold on. Another whack against

the marble and this time something bigger broke.
Raul heard the snap and took advantage of the moment. He popped Kelman's wrist one more time,
then twisted it. The gun fell free. Unable to get to
it himself, Raul did the next best thing. He batted
the pistol with his elbow and sent it spinning into
a corner. He wouldn't be able to reach it, but neither would Kelman.

Using the opportunity to twist away, Kelman
jumped to his feet. His wrist dangled uselessly before him, but he suddenly lunged forward. Raul
followed his movements with his eyes, his heart
stopping as he saw what had happened. The gun
had lodged beneath the tub, caught by one of the
old-fashioned legs. In one quick motion, Kelman
bent down and picked it up with his good hand,
swinging around to fire.

Raul searched for a weapon. Strangely enough,
he saw a cane lying in a corner. He didn't stop to
wonder about it; he picked it up and gripped it with
both hands. The gleaming silver top hissed through
the air with the force of his swing.

It connected with Kelman's head. And the other
man went down without a sound.

Raul turned instantly to Emma. She was a crumpled ball in the corner, her limbs splayed, her body
slack. Then he saw the empty bottles and understood. He lifted her head gently. "Emma? Emma,
can you hear me?"

KAY DAVID
289

Her head lolled sideways and his heart almost stopped. He started to scream her name again, but then he saw her throat move, saw the faint pulse at the base of her neck. Too slow to be okay, too faint to last long. He picked her up and ran from the room.

Two DAYS LATER, it seemed like a dream. A very bad dream. Emma's throat still burned from the attentions of the doctors, but it wasn't important. Her children were safe, she was alive.

And Kelman was dead.

The Bolivian police had been exceedingly co-operative. Emma knew it had more to do with Raul's friend Wendy Fortune and her position than it had to do with the situation. The consul had gotten involved, and everything had been handled so smoothly Emma had been shocked.

Chris had been happy to have the whole thing resolved without the bank's name being mentioned. He'd had no idea of Emma's machinations. No idea that she'd rigged Kelman's account. No idea she'd planned everything. Including Kelman's death.

She wondered now what she'd been thinking. Had she really been prepared to kill him? She'd fired, yes, but she'd missed. Had that been deliberate? She'd never know now and she wasn't really sure she wanted to.

Sitting on the terrace at the back of the house, Emma held the portable phone to her ear and closed her eyes, the sunshine on her face warm and healing, the voices she was listening to, even more so. Jake was babbling about catching a fish, and Sarah was saying something about a sand castle and the princess who lived inside it. Emma let them talk. She didn't care if the conversation made sense. They were perfectly fine and thought they'd simply had a great vacation at Gulf Shores the week before. After another minute, Todd came on the line and shooed them away.

"Emma, you gonna be all right? Were you hurt bad?" Someone hearing his question might have thought he was concerned; Emma knew it meant just the opposite. Todd would be thrilled if she died and he didn't have to factor her into his plans anymore.

"I'll make it." Her voice was whiskey hoarse and raw. It was painful to talk, and as she spoke, she moved, then winced. Her whole body was bruised, black and blue marks everywhere she looked. Kelman's last legacy. "I need a few days to rest, that's all."

"The man who killed this Kelman fellow. You know him well?"

"He's a friend," she answered in a neutral voice.

Raul had come by to see her numerous times,

but Emma had been so out of it Reina had sent him away each time. Emma had heard their voices downstairs, though. Reina had told him about Emma's hours in jail. Raul's reply had been too low to hear. They still hadn't talked, but when they did, Emma didn't know what she'd say.

Todd broke into her thoughts, and the minute he spoke, Emma knew she was in trouble. He had that gloating, I'm-in-the-catbird-seat kind of tone to his voice. "Listen here, Emma, I want you to know, I'm very upset about this situation. You have, once again, put our children in danger, and I don't intend to let this slip by. I've already talked to the lawyers, in fact, and we're considerin' some kind of action."

A clamp tightened around her heart, making it hard for her to breath. It had nothing to do with her injuries. "Some kind of action? What does that mean?"

"It means we know you're up to your same old tricks. You're bein' irresponsible and not thinkin' about your children." He took a self-important breath, dragging out the moment. "It means I'm gonna have to do something about this again, just like I did before."

Through her fear, Emma heard his words. She wasn't surprised by his reaction, but instead of the defeat she usually let overcome her when he talked like this, a new emotion suffused her. Anger. Total and complete anger.

Her fury mounted, and when Todd finally ran out of steam, she spoke through clenched teeth. "I handled this situation the best way I knew how, and frankly, I did a much better job taking care of it than you ever could have done. If you think you're going to use what happened to your advantage, you—and your lawyers—have got another think coming."

He made a scoffing sound. "You don't know what you're talking about, Emma. You screwed up—again—and the judge will see right through this, just like he did before."

"I don't think so."

"You don't think so." He mocked her, speaking in a higher voice. "And just what makes you think that, Emma Lou? Nothing's changed, you know."

"You're wrong," she said quietly. "*I've* changed. I'm a different person than I was the last time we spoke, and I'm not taking your crap anymore."

He started to sputter a response, but she didn't give him a chance to finish it. His entire life he'd gotten what he wanted by using his name and his family and his money, but deep down inside, he had nothing. No courage, no heart, no strength. None of the qualities Raul possessed, she realized. None of what she needed.

Fueled by a sudden determination, she spoke again, her voice grim and gritty. "I made the biggest mistake of my life when I let you take my kids and run me out of town. I don't know what in hell I thought I was doing, but I can tell you one thing. I *never* should have let you get away with it. And you won't again, I can promise you that."

"You're full of—"

"I'm coming home, Todd." She sat up straighter and ignored the pain that ripped through her body. "I'm coming home, and I'm going to fight you for those kids, and I'm going to win, because I'm going to have help this time. I won't be alone, so don't think your old tactics are going to work anymore."

She didn't let him reply. Her heart pumping, her hands shaking, Emma hit the disconnect button with a decisive click as a righteous courage washed over her. She would defeat Todd. She would!

Just as she had the thought, she heard steps coming up the walk. Still jumpy, she tensed, then when she saw who it was, she tensed even more.

He stopped beside the gate. He had on a white shirt that contrasted with the brown of his skin, and soft black pants with loafers and no socks. The afternoon sun glinted off his black hair. He looked more handsome and sensual than he ever had, and a shot of pure electric desire moved inside her as she met his dark eyes. But immediately Emma realized there was something different about Raul.

The tightness around his eyes was gone, his stance looser, his body language completely unlike what it had been before. At his side, his hands hung open and unfisted; his walk as he'd approached was fluid. The single thing that remained from before was his intensity—that stark ripple of energy that always surrounded him—but even this had a different feel to it.

Then she realized why. She was seeing who Raul had been before. The man he'd been all those years ago, the man he'd been when they each had yet to be shaped by the pain they now felt.

He reached around and unlatched the gate—the hinge was fixed now—closing it behind him before heading to where she sat. He stopped just short of her chair, the space between them more significant to her than it should be. She tried to analyze his expression then gave up.

"¿Cómo estás, Emmita?"

It was the first time she'd ever heard him speak the language, she realized with a start. His accent was soft, and he slurred the words with a Texan-style beat.

In the silence of the hot afternoon, everything waited. The only sound between them was the buzz of the bees as they worked around the bird-of-paradise bushes.

"How are you?" He repeated, this time in English.

"I'm fine." Taking a deep breath and an even bigger chance, she met his dark gaze. "Now that you're here."

He covered the space between them in a heartbeat. Dropping to his knees on the terrace beside her chair, he took her hand in his. "Do you mean that?"

"Absolutely." She gripped his fingers. She couldn't hold them as tightly as she wanted to, but he got the message, she was sure. "You saved my life, Raul. I can never, ever repay you."

Above his stormy stare, his eyebrows knit. "Is that the only reason?"

"It's enough."

He shook his head. "Not for me, it isn't. I need more than that from you."

"Then how about this?" She leaned toward him and cupped his face in her hands, her fingertips caressing him. He responded automatically, moving toward her. Her eyes locked on his and she proceeded to kiss him. Deeply.

When she finally pulled back, Emma was surer than ever she was doing the right thing. She only prayed Raul felt the same way. Whether he did or not, she had to try, she'd already decided. It was time to start living her life in the present, instead of the past.

"Is that a good enough reason for you?"

His face only inches from hers, he spoke softly and shocked her. "No, I'm sorry. There's only one answer that will do. As great as your kisses are, I still need more." Placing his hand on her neck, he rubbed his thumb at the base of her throat. The touch was so gentle she barely felt it, yet it reverberated deep inside her.

"I love you," he said simply. "And I need to know you love me, too. Can you do that, Emma? After everything that's happened between us?"

Her heart sung, but she spoke cautiously, unable to accept the possibility before her. "Maybe I should be the one asking you that. I should have told you what Kelman was doing. If I'd done that one little thing, none of this would have happened."

"I'm not sure I agree." His eyes turned blacker. "I've had a lot of time these past few days to think about it. The way it ended was inevitable."

"What do you mean?"

His hand tightened against her neck. Once he'd realized the truth of it, the knowledge of how he'd felt had begun to eat Raul up. For the past two days—the past two tortured days—he'd been killing himself with the knowledge. Emma was too good, too strong, too…perfect to love someone like him. He had to tell her the truth, though. When he was an old man and remembering his past, not telling her this and taking a chance would be the one thing he wouldn't be able to stand.

"I had thought all along that what I wanted to do was ruin Kelman. To take his money and turn his life to shit like he'd done to me. When I came here that night, I realized I wanted more." His mouth tightened. "I wanted him dead, Emma. I *wanted* to kill him, and I knew that when I went up those stairs."

"You don't carry that burden by yourself, Raul. I felt the same way."

There was something about her voice that made him stop and look at her. In her hazel eyes was a depth of emotion he'd never seen before. It chilled him, but he actually understood. That didn't change things, though.

Raul shook his head. "Maybe so, but not like I did, and you need to understand the truth of it if we're going any farther. What Kelman did changed me. I spent five years in a federal prison. I turned hard. I'm not the man I was."

She reached over and put her hand on his arm. One pink nail had been broken off, down to the quick. The knuckle was bruised and cut, too. Lifting her finger to his mouth, he kissed it gently. She spoke as his lips touched her skin and his heart stopped.

"You *aren't* who you were."

Before he could speak again, she continued,

"No one could be the same after that. I'm not who I was a week ago, either." Her voice held regret, even sorrow, then it grew stronger. "But the person you are now is the person I love. And I always will."

A kind of feeling he'd never expected to have again swelled inside him. His throat burned with the suddenness of it all. "Are you sure?"

"Absolutely." Her eyes warmed. "I love you and I think I've felt that way ever since that day at the orphanage. Seeing you there, with all the kids, something happened to me then." She paused. "But the problem I had—with the pills and everything—that doesn't bother you?"

"You had a problem and you fixed it. What's there to worry about now?" He wrapped his arms around her in a possessive hug. It was tender, but it said everything else that needed to be said. He pulled back only when she spoke once more.

"There is one more thing, though…"

"We can deal with it. Whatever it is."

"It's my children. They're always going to come first, Raul, and that's something you'll have to deal with. First, in this case, means I'm going back to the States to fight for them. Nothing else matters to me until I get that straightened out." Her fingers tightened on his arm. "Can you wait?"

"I'll go back with you," he said instantly. "I may not hold a license anymore, but I *am* still an attorney. I could help you, if you like…if you'll let me.''

Emma's eyes filled with tears. They spilled down her cheeks, and Raul reached over to wipe them away with his thumb. His offer was exactly what she'd hoped for when she'd been talking to Todd, but she couldn't have asked—he had to volunteer, just as he had.

''You'd do that for me?'' she asked.

''I'd do anything for you, Emma. You should know that by now.''

She nodded weakly.

''But you have to do something in return for me.''

She lifted her brimming eyes to his and gripped his hands. ''Anything. You name it and it's yours.''

''Marry me,'' he said quietly. ''Be my wife. Have my children. Give me a life and love me forever.''

She didn't speak, but she didn't need to. She leaned forward and pressed her lips to his. The kiss was as soft and as sweet as the first time they'd come together. In its healing warmth, their past faded, then disappeared, the pain nothing more than ashes, the hurt forgiven. The future rose before them.

HARLEQUIN®
SUPERROMANCE®

You are now entering

WELCOME TO
RIVERBEND
POPULATION
8793

Riverbend…the kind of place where everyone knows your name—and your business. Riverbend…home of the River Rats—a group of small-town sons and daughters who've been friends since high school.

The Rats are all grown up now. Living their lives and learning that some days are good and some days aren't—and that you can get through anything as long as you have your friends.

Starting in July 2000, Harlequin Superromance brings you Riverbend—six books about the River Rats and the Midwest town they live in.

BIRTHRIGHT by Judith Arnold (July 2000)
THAT SUMMER THING by Pamela Bauer (August 2000)
HOMECOMING by Laura Abbot (September 2000)
LAST-MINUTE MARRIAGE by Marisa Carroll (October 2000)
A CHRISTMAS LEGACY by Kathryn Shay (November 2000)

Available wherever Harlequin books are sold.

HARLEQUIN®
Makes any time special ™

Visit us at www.eHarlequin.com

HSRIVER

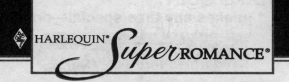

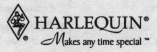

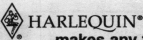

HARLEQUIN®
makes any time special—online...

eHARLEQUIN.com

your romantic
books

- ♥ Shop online! Visit Shop eHarlequin and discover a wide selection of new releases and classic favorites at great discounted prices.

- ♥ Read our daily and weekly Internet exclusive serials, and participate in our interactive novel in the reading room.

- ♥ Ever dreamed of being a writer? Enter your chapter for a chance to become a featured author in our Writing Round Robin novel.

your romantic
life

- ♥ Check out our feature articles on dating, flirting and other important romance topics and get your daily love dose with tips on how to keep the romance alive every day.

• • • • • • •

your
community

- ♥ Have a Heart-to-Heart with other members about the latest books and meet your favorite authors.

- ♥ Discuss your romantic dilemma in the Tales from the Heart message board.

your romantic
escapes

- ♥ Learn what the stars have in store for you with our daily Passionscopes and weekly Erotiscopes.

- ♥ Get the latest scoop on your favorite royals in Royal Romance.